PAWS AND EFFECT

A MYSTIC NOTCH COZY MYSTERY

LEIGHANN DOBBS

ALSO BY LEIGHANN DOBBS

KATE DIAMOND
Adventure/Suspense Series

Hidden Agemda
Ancient Hiss Story

MYSTIC NOTCH
Cats & Magic Cozy Mystery Series

Ghostly Paws
A Spirited Tail
A Mew To A Kill

BLACKMOORE SISTERS
Cozy Mystery Series

Dead Wrong
Dead & Buried
Dead Tide
Buried Secrets
Deadly Intentions
A Grave Mistake

MOOSEAMUCK ISLAND
Cozy Mystery Series

A Zen For Murder

LEXY BAKER
Cozy Mystery Series

Lexy Baker Cozy Mystery Series
Boxed Set Vol 1 (Books 1-4)

Or buy the books separately:

Killer Cupcakes (Book 1)
Dying For Danish (Book 2)
Murder, Money and Marzipan (Book 3)
3 Bodies and a Biscotti (Book 4)
Brownies, Bodies & Bad Guys (Book 5)
Bake, Battle & Roll (Book 6)
Wedded Blintz (Book 7)
Scones, Skulls & Scams (Book 8)
Ice Cream Murder (Book 9)
Mummified Meringues (Book 10)
Brutal Brulee (Book 11 - Novella)

CONTEMPORARY ROMANCE

Sweet Escapes
Reluctant Romance

PAWS AND
EFFECT

PROLOGUE

November 12, 1656
Mystic Notch, New Hampshire

Hester Warren's heart pounded in her chest as she ran through the dark woods. The full moon cast flickers of light through bare tree limbs that poked up into the sky like the crooked fingers of a skeleton, but Hester didn't need the moonlight. She knew exactly where she was going.

Beneath her booted feet, newly fallen leaves crunched. Her breath came in quick puffs of condensation. Her black wool cloak flapped out behind her, allowing a gust of crisp, cold air to slap at her body. She grabbed at the edge of the cloak with her left hand, pulling it closed and wrapping the rough fabric tightly around her.

The silver box she clutched in her right hand weighed heavy with doubt and responsibility.

Was she doing the right thing?

Hester wondered how things had gotten so out of hand. She thought they'd successfully diverted all the suspicions of witchcraft to Salem, Massachusetts, strategically keeping attention away from Mystic Notch where magic was most powerful.

But somehow Miles Danforth and Nathaniel Phipps had taken up the charge here. She'd heard rumblings that she was next to be accused. And if that happened, she couldn't let them take possession of what was in the box.

Her cat, Obsidian, ran silently beside her, his jet black fur nearly invisible in the dark night. She didn't have time to go far. If what Goody St. Onge had told her was true, they could come for her tonight and she had to make sure the box was safe … if it fell into the wrong hands, there was no telling what evil deeds they would do with the contents.

The giant oak tree loomed up ahead of her and she turned to the east, judged a distance of thirty feet and then dropped to her knees.

She clawed at the dirt with her fingernails, releasing the moldy scent of wet earth and decaying leaves. Obsidian, ever the obedient companion, used his powerful claws to help.

The wind whistled in Hester's ears as she dug. She no longer noticed the chill of the air, or the dampness of the ground seeping into her knees because her entire being was focused on the task at hand.

The box must be protected above all.

Hester knew the forest like the back of her hand. She spent a lot of time here, but usually during the day. Now, as her fingernails scratched into the earth, she noticed with a hollow sadness that the daytime sounds of the birdcalls she most enjoyed in the forest were absent. No mournful cry of the mourning dove, no twitter from the red-breasted robin and no chirping melodies of mockingbirds could be heard— just cold silence and the sound of her own ragged breath as she dug at a frantic pace.

She was glad her nighttime visit would soon be over and longed for it to be the next day when she could venture out in the golden sunshine and listen to those daytime birdcalls again.

When the hole was deep enough, she laid the silver box carefully inside. Her fingers traced its outline, lingering over the contours of the newt-shaped design embossed into the shiny, moon-lit surface.

Then she pushed the loose dirt back into the hole, listening to the dull thud as it hit the top of the box. She pressed the earth down, and covered it with leaves so as to obliterate any trace of the ground having been disturbed.

Obsidian's golden eyes glowed brightly as he watched her. Something rustled behind them. Hester's stomach clenched as she whirled around, her breath whooshing out when she saw nothing but trees.

She knew she had to hurry back, but still took a moment to stroke Obsidian's soft fur. She had no idea what the next few days would bring. Maybe nothing, but if the worst happened, she had to make sure the box was protected.

"If anything happens to me, you must guard this box."

Obsidian's golden eyes blinked at her with an intelligence that telegraphed the cat knew what she was requesting.

3

Hester was overcome with worry for the box and the cat. Miles Danforth's hatred of cats was well known and he'd recently started a campaign to purge Mystic Notch of all felines, stating that they were the instruments of witches and carried disease and destruction. She knew Obsidian had ways of taking care of himself—she just hoped they were more powerful than Miles' hatred.

But she didn't have time to dwell on the cat's safety or even her own. The most important thing was the box whose care had been entrusted to her family for generations. She was the last one left to protect it.

Was burying it here the right thing to do? She had no idea, but at twenty-one years of age and with no money to speak of, she didn't have many options. She'd done the best thing she could think of. It would have to be good enough.

She spun around and hurried back toward her cabin. The lone light from the candle she'd left lit on the doorstep acted like a homing beacon. Its warm glow soothed her and beckoned her home.

She hoped she was just being paranoid and the whole witchcraft frenzy would blow over and she could dig up the box and go back to life as she knew it. Then she remembered how Miles' accusing eyes were always watching her and icy fingers of premonition danced up her spine.

Relief washed over her as she reached her cabin. Her right foot flew onto the granite step and her hand reached out toward the iron latch of her door.

She was home. Safe.

But even as her pale hand curled around the latch, a large, calloused hand clamped around her wrist in a painful vise-grip, wrenching hers away from the door.

She whipped her head to the right and looked straight into the dark, blank eyes of Miles Danforth. He towered over her, his thin, shoulder-length black hair whipping in the wind. Her heart jerked in her chest at the look of triumph on his face.

She tried to pull her wrist away. Another hand clamped onto her other wrist. Nathaniel Phipps.

"I do not think you will be going in there." Miles sneered at her as he yanked her away from the cabin. "Your sorcery will not help you now."

"Let go of me!" She tried to pull her arms away from the men, but they were too strong. She twisted and kicked, but they easily dragged her away from her home.

She chanced one backward glance to see Obsidian pacing worriedly in front of the door. Their eyes locked in a knowing glance as Miles Danforth said, "Hester Warren, you are under arrest for the crime of witchcraft."

CHAPTER 1

Present Day
Mystic Notch, New Hampshire

Willa Chance looked out with mixed feelings at the clearing slated to become the new home of the Mystic Notch Historical Society.

She loved the wooded area with its mature landscape and centuries-old trees, like the giant oak she now stood under. It seemed a shame to cut down those trees to erect a building, especially on a bright, sunny spring day where birds chirped and chipmunks rustled in the leaves. But there was no stopping it. Already a bulldozer sat at the edge of the property and several tarps covered various other types of equipment.

The aroma of honeysuckle brought a slow smile to her face and she tried to forget about the construction equipment while she tried to block out the droning voice of Rebecca Devon-Smyth, the mayor. Rebecca's speech about the new historical society building included a long-winded history of her ancestors' important contributions to the town of Mystic Notch.

Willa preferred to listen to the birds—the mournful cry of the mourning dove, the twitter of the red-breasted robin and the chirping melodies of the mockingbirds.

Her heart squeezed as she realized some of the very trees these birds lived in would be sacrificed for the new building. How many nests with newly laid eggs waiting to hatch would be destroyed?

Yet, the area was perfect for the historical society which was currently crowded into a small room in the town hall. As a seller of antique and used books, Willa loved the idea of moving the historical society to a bigger space, especially since the bigger space would allow them to open a museum that would include antique books.

As a member of the historical society herself, Willa had a great respect for history, especially that of Mystic Notch, and she knew the historical society desperately needed to expand. The town had voted to put a new building right on this site, which was incredibly appropriate as it had been the home of one of Mystic Notch's most infamous residents, Hester Warren.

According to the very sketchy town records, Hester had been accused of witchcraft and burned at the stake in 1656. Her land had been seized by the town and lain unused ever since. Some said the land was haunted by Hester, but Willa did not think that was true. If it *was* haunted, she probably would have seen Hester by now since ghosts had the annoying habit of manifesting themselves in front of her.

No one knew exactly where Hester's house had stood. The records had been lost long ago. All they had was an old deed with the boundaries of the small property. So the town surveyor had chosen the best place to site the building and here Willa was at the ground-breaking ceremony along with the mayor, several members of the historical society and a variety of onlookers.

One of these was her sister, Augusta—or Gus as Willa called her—who was the current sheriff of Mystic Notch. Gus had her blonde hair pulled up into a severe bun, which Willa suspected Gus thought made her look more authoritative.

Beside Gus was Willa's on-again-off-again boyfriend Eddie Striker, the sheriff of the neighboring County. He and Gus often helped each other out on investigations. Willa wasn't sure why he was here now, but his handsome, square-jawed face and deep gray eyes were welcome sights, no matter what the reason.

A handful of townspeople, none of whom seemed to be paying attention to Rebecca's boring speech, stood in clusters around the clearing.

Willa's eyes drifted around the small crowd as Rebecca droned on. Across from Willa, Gus and Striker looked official in their brown sheriff's uniforms, their feet shoulder-width apart arms clasped behind their backs. Striker was a full foot taller than Willa's petite sister and his broad shoulders made Gus look even more like a Barbie doll than usual.

Striker winked at her.

Willa blushed.

Gus scowled at both of them.

Rebecca finished her speech and there was a round of muted applause.

Elizabeth Post, an aging crone with wrinkly hands and a nest of hair died a bold, unnatural red, stood beside Rebecca. Elizabeth was the head of the historical society, and thus had possession of the groundbreaking shovel—a small, gold-colored tool which Willa thought was much too flimsy to dig a hole. Elizabeth handed the ineffective shovel to Rebecca, who accepted it with an exaggerated flourish.

A hush fell over the crowd. Rebecca poised the shovel in mid-air, pausing with a smile plastered on her face for pictures as the heels of her stilettos slowly sank into the soft ground.

Once the camera clicking stopped, Rebecca plunged the shovel into the ground.

Clink.

Rebecca's Botoxed brow tried to mash together as the shovel hit something halfway in.

"What was that?" Elizabeth asked.

Rebecca shrugged, scooped some dirt up with the shovel, tossed it beside the hole and plunged the shovel in again for another scoop of dirt. Then she paused, leaning forward to look into the hole.

Elizabeth bent her head over the hole as well.

"There's something in here," Rebecca said.

Willa had moved closer to the hole along with the rest of the crowd and she peered over someone's shoulder at the corner of something shiny and silver that lay half-buried in the dirt.

Elizabeth grabbed the shovel from Rebecca and scraped more dirt from the hole. Then she squatted down, her knees cracking alarmingly. She reached a claw-like hand into the hole and pulled out an ornate, silver box, like an eagle plucking a salmon from a river.

"What the heck?" Cordelia Deering, one of Willa's senior-citizen bookstore regulars who showed up promptly every morning with coffee and gossip, looked quizzically at the box. Beside her, her twin sister Hattie wore a matching lemon and lime polyester pantsuit and had an identical quizzical expression.

Elizabeth turned the box to study every side. Willa could see it was in good shape. She couldn't tell how long it had been buried there, but it looked old. The edges were fancy and on the top was some sort of embossed reptile.

"What's in it?" Oscar Danforth asked in a breathless voice.

Elizabeth slowly opened the lid.

Willa craned to see what was inside.

Oscar reached his pale hand out toward the box. Before he could get it inside, Rebecca grabbed the box out of Elizabeth's hand and snapped the lid shut. "Not so fast. This is town property, Danforth."

Oscar snatched his hand back and frowned at her.

"It should go in the museum," Elizabeth objected.

"I wonder if it belonged to Hester Warren?" Hattie asked.

"If it did, then by rights it's town property," Rebecca said. "Her home and property were taken to pay for the trial as she had no money."

"But there's no way to know if it was hers," Willa pointed out.

"But what do you think it's *for*?" Cordelia asked.

"Some kind of magic, maybe? She *was* a witch." Hattie's cornflower-blue eyes twinkled with mischief as the crowd tittered with nervous laughter.

Bing Thorndike, an aging magician who was like an uncle to Willa and another one of her bookstore regulars, cleared his throat. "No matter whose it is, it could be a valuable part of Mystic Notch history. We should make sure it's put somewhere for safekeeping."

"Yeah, like the police station." Gus held out her hand for the box. "We'll keep it there until the thirty days is up."

Bing furrowed his white brow in Gus' direction "Thirty days?"

"Yes. That's the law. When property is found and turned in to the police, a public notice goes out in the paper and the owner has thirty days to claim it. If it's not claimed, the finder gets to keep it."

"Wait a minute, I don't think this qualifies as *found*," Oscar said.

"Why not?" Gus asked. "We *found* it right here in the ground. We don't know how long it's been here. Someone could have stolen it last week and buried it here."

"That's right," Striker added. "We'll look through the listings of stolen goods to see if it's on there, then after that we need to give the rightful owner a chance to claim it."

"If no one claims it, then I'll be happy to turn it over to the finder after that," Gus said.

Elizabeth fisted her hands on her hips. "And just who is the *finder* in this case."

Gus tilted her head to consider the question. "Well, we *are* here for the official groundbreaking of the historical society building and museum. So I say it would probably go to the museum."

"I don't know about that," Danforth cut in. "This looks suspiciously like something I've seen in my ancestors' papers. I think this might belong my family."

"Not so fast." Elizabeth held up a gnarled hand. "You have to prove that fair and square. Until then, I think it should go on display at the society." She reached out to take the box from Gus, but Gus pulled it back, cradling it under her arm like a football.

"Oh no. It's going to the police station. You each have thirty days to bring your proof that you're the rightful owner."

Striker had gravitated over to Willa's side. They were in an 'on-again' phase of their relationship, which suited Willa just fine especially since the mere presence of him made her body temperature rise a few degrees. Or maybe it was just the hot flashes that had plagued her once she turned fifty. Either way, she liked having him next to her.

She glanced back down at the hole the box had been in and something caught her eye. Her heart kicked. The bleached-out white object was something that shouldn't be there—a bone.

"What's that?" Striker asked, following her gaze.

"Looks like a bone."

They bent down, the silver box forgotten. With relief, Willa noticed the bones were too small to be human.

"These are tiny." Striker gently pushed away the dirt to reveal a small skull and thin rib bones. "Cat bones."

Willa's heart tugged. "What would cat bones be doing out here?"

"Probably an animal got it. Mountain lion or coyote," Striker said.

"It must have been one of the feral cats."

Mystic Notch was home to a large population of feral cats who several town members, including Willa, volunteered to keep fed and sheltered. Unfortunately, there were many town members who wanted to hurt those cats. They saw them as wild animals and a nuisance. For this reason, the location of the various shelters that Willa and the others used for the cats was kept a closely guarded secret.

This month the cats were being sheltered in an old building behind the church that was down the street from Willa's shop on Maine Street. They took turns feeding the cats, getting them spayed and neutered and trying to socialize them so that they could be adopted out to forever homes.

Willa knew the life of a feral cat was fraught with danger. Any number of animals, including humans, could inflict harm on them. When she visited the feral cat shelter, she always had an eye out to see if all the known ferals were accounted for. She grieved when one turned up missing and hated to think the bones might belong to one of those cats.

"Maybe," Striker said. "But not recently. It looks like they've been here for a while. They're picked clean."

Striker got a small tarp from the construction area and Willa's heart melted at how gently he removed the bones from the dirt and placed them on the tarp.

"We'll give it a proper burial." Striker folded the tarp neatly.

"Well, this is certainly the most interesting ground-breaking ceremony to hit Mystic Notch," Hattie said over Striker's shoulder as she watched him.

Striker seemed distracted. Willa noticed him looking into the woods as if something was there, but when Willa followed his gaze, she saw nothing. He looked up at Hattie, then down at the small tarp, his mouth set in a grim line. "Somehow, I have a feeling things are about to get much more interesting."

CHAPTER 2

Sunlight poured through the bookstore window, heating Pandora's sleek, gray fur to a perfect ninety-eight degrees. She snuggled down into her soft, shearling cat bed and soaked in the warmth like a sunbather on the Rivera.

Pandora's life was nearly perfect. As the official bookstore cat at *Last Chance Books*, Pandora enjoyed certain luxuries of which the sunny spot in the store's window and luxury cat bed were two.

If only she could train her human, Willa, better. With a sigh, she slit one greenish-gold eye open so she could observe Willa and Striker, who were engaged in conversation across the room.

Pandora normally preferred to ignore the humans. Their mundane daily tasks were of no interest to her. She did, however, keep half an eye on them as she was sworn to protect them. For the most part, no protection was necessary, but there had been times when Pandora and the cats of Mystic Notch—who, like her, were sworn to protect humans—had been called upon to go above and beyond to ensure the balance of power stayed on the side of good.

The humans went about their business, blissfully unaware of the lengths the cats had gone to and the cats preferred to keep it that way. It wouldn't do to have humans knowing what was *really* going on.

As she watched Willa and Striker, she noticed the conversation seemed awkward—strained, somehow. She opened her eye a little wider. It was as if Striker was distracted, trying to keep Willa away from something and Willa was suspicious, noticing Striker's strange behavior.

Pandora raised her awareness just a tad to listen to the conversation. Normally, she found their talk to be excruciatingly boring. She hardly ever bothered to listen because in doing so, she had to expend extra energy to translate the humans' inferior mode of communication, but their unusual body language had piqued her interest.

They were talking about some box and a pile of bones. Yawn. But it wasn't what they were saying that was of interest. It was the way Striker was *acting*.

Now that she was paying attention, she could sense something very odd in his demeanor. She liked the man and thought he was perfect for Willa. In fact, she happened to know that the two of them were made for each other, even if they had yet to figure that out.

One of the things she liked most about Striker was his kindness. Though he was a tough guy on the outside, she knew he was a teddy bear inside. He'd even saved her life once, rushing her to the veterinarian when she had been gravely wounded. Another time, he'd cared for her when Willa had been wounded.

He was a good guy. Plus, he was a looker, at least by human standards. Pandora herself preferred something with more fur, but for female humans, Striker was definitely a man any woman would be happy to sink their claws into.

Other than Striker, Willa and Pandora, the bookstore was empty. Pandora usually liked to take this quiet time to nap, but the humans' curious behavior had gotten the best of her.

She dialed her awareness up another notch. Cats' senses were much more powerful than humans'. Pandora usually kept hers running on low in order not to become overwhelmed by sensory data that would zap her energy and require even more napping time than her usual eighteen hours.

As she heightened her senses, details of her surroundings came into focus like the sharpening of the landscape upon turning the knob on a pair of binoculars.

The musty smell of old books, mingled with the Orange Glo cleaner that Willa used on the oak bookcases and counter, pervaded the air. The creak of the old, pine floorboards, normally barely audible, sounded like firecrackers every time Willa and Striker changed position. The cat bed became even more soft and luxurious and the tiny molecules still left on her tongue brought back the taste of the turkey and greens Fancy Feast breakfast Pandora had chowed down earlier that morning. On the counter, Pandora could see waves of blue, red and yellow energy flowing out from Willa's computer.

Striker's movements suggested that he was trying to keep Willa from seeing something that was happening behind her back. But Pandora could see nothing ... not on this plane, anyway. And, judging from Willa's reaction, she couldn't see anything either, but was confused over Striker's jerky movements and strange body language.

Pandora figured there must be a reason for his weird behavior, so she turned her awareness up another notch and that's when she saw it.

Behind Willa stood a ghost. Pandora still wasn't at full awareness, but she could make out the barely visible figure of a female with a long cloak that swirled about as she gestured wildly, trying to get Striker's attention.

Pandora noticed with amusement that Striker was trying very hard to ignore the ghost and not let on to Willa that he saw something. Willa was smart, though. She kept looking over her shoulder, sensing exactly where Striker did *not* want her to look. Apparently, Willa could not see the ghost.

Pandora thought this was hysterical, because she knew that Willa also saw ghosts and took great pains to hide that fact from Striker. Neither one of them knew that the other had the strange ability to see the dead, and both of them had been trying to hide it for a long time.

Pandora couldn't say she blamed them. It was not normal to see ghosts. Even among cats the ability was not bestowed on all. But whereas in cats it was considered a special gift, in humans it was shunned. Pandora was proud to have the gift and even better, she could see ghosts on all planes. Willa and Striker could only see them on one plane—and not the same plane, either, which explained why Striker never saw the ghosts that frequented the bookstore and why Willa could not see this ghost now.

The hairs along Pandora's spine tingled with electricity. This might be something she should pay attention to. She heightened her senses even further, bringing the sketchy outline of the ghost into focus. Pandora rarely notched her senses up this far. It took too much of her energy. She would have to spend a lot of time lying on Willa's keyboard or standing in front of the monitor to charge up her energy stores.

Willa and Striker were still rambling on about the box and bones, but Pandora had little interest in their conversation. She was busy watching the ghost. By the way it was gesturing, it really wanted some help. Now that she could see her better, she realized she was a very old ghost, dressed in garb from centuries ago. She must have been haunting this plane for a long time. Pandora knew a ghost would have to have a pretty good reason to stick around that long.

"Pssst." Pandora heard a strange noise from near the swirling ghost and cocked her head, angling her ear so as to hear it better. Then she saw it peeking out from behind the ghost's swirling cape.

A ghost cat! And it was beckoning Pandora over.

Ghost cats were incredibly rare. Cats usually had no reason to hang around on this plane and preferred to pass over to the other side immediately after serving their nine lives. Pandora didn't know why any would stay here. She heard the other side was quite beautiful with a colorful rainbow bridge and filled with flowers and fields and lots of mice for the taking. A cat would have to have a powerful reason not to be lured over to the other side right away.

Pandora was intrigued by the ghost cat. She hunched up her back and extended her front legs in a stretch, then jumped down from the window and trotted over to inspect the feline apparition.

Her journey caused Willa and Striker to pause. Striker frowned down at her, glancing from her to the ghost cat then up at Willa. Willa was also frowning at her and Pandora figured her actions of trotting to sit in the middle of nowhere to look at nothing must seem pretty random to the human. Then again, she often did random things just to keep Willa confused.

The ghost smiled when she saw Pandora and bent down to pat her on top of the head. Striker's eyes widened and he gave Pandora a quizzical look. Pandora decided to freak him out, so she looked up at him and winked.

"What's going on?" Willa asked.

"Nothing. Nothing at all," Striker said quickly, causing Willa to cast another suspicious glance behind her.

"You're acting kind of strange," Willa said.

"I need coffee," Striker replied. "I didn't get one before the ceremony." He pulled Willa over to the desk and away from the ghost who just followed him anyway, all the while blathering on about some box that she needed him to protect.

Pandora addressed the ghost cat. "What's that all about?" She jerked her head toward the two humans and the ghost.

The cat shrugged. "Humans. Who can explain their strange behavior?"

"No one," Pandora agreed. "But ghosts usually behave that way for only one reason. They want something."

"Oh, *that*. Right. My human was entrusted with a very important silver box. She has waited on this plane of existence all these centuries to make sure it does not get into the wrong hands."

"Why wait so long?" Pandora asked.

"It was hidden, but has recently surfaced. The human over there has access to it."

Pandora's whiskers twitched. "You mean Striker?"

The cat nodded. "Yes, the male."

"What are *you* doing here?" Pandora asked. "I've never seen a ghost cat before and I've seen my share of ghosts."

"Yep, that's right. I'm a rare, cool cat. Not many of us have the guts to tough it out here on this plane." He glanced over at the human ghost and his expression softened. "My name is Obsidian. The ghost was my human. She left me in charge of the box, which I guarded religiously. Unfortunately, my nine lives were lived out and I could no longer guard it. I was reunited on this plane with my human and I decided to stick around and help her out. She's determined to make sure the box doesn't fall into the wrong hands. She cannot rest until it is safe with the right person."

"And you think Striker is that person?" Pandora asked.

Obsidian glanced over at the humans. "No, but he has access to the box, so he can at least get it to the right person. But he does not seem like he wants to listen to my human." His eyes flicked back to Pandora, sparking a brilliant golden color. "You are young, still wet behind the ears, but perhaps you can help."

Pandora backed up a step and looked at Obsidian skeptically. The challenge in his words had her hackles raised. Sure, she was only on her first life, which was young in cat terms, but she was pretty smart and fully capable of taking care of things. She didn't mind helping out, especially if it was something important, but she wasn't convinced this *was* important. Besides, she didn't know this ghost cat and wasn't sure if she should trust him.

She narrowed her eyes. "What do you mean? How can I help?"

"The contents of the box would have disastrous effects if it got in the wrong hands. It can make evil more powerful. I think you do not want that to happen." He narrowed his eyes. "Am I correct?"

Pandora sat on her haunches and casually licked her paw, rubbing it behind her ear slowly. "Sure. Who wants powerful evil? No one. But I don't know what you think I can do to help."

Obsidian sized her up. "You can persuade your human and the other cats to come to the cause. The evil ones want to harm the humans through the cats ... especially one powerful cat in particular."

Pandora's paw froze halfway from mouth to ear. Was he talking about the cat they had recently saved from the clutches of the bad guys? The two-faced cat that had been written about in the old scrolls?

A sense of doom flooded through her. "Tell me more about this box. What is in it? How can it harm us and what can I do to stop it?"

"As you know, there are humans who would have evil prevail, and those who would have good prevail. You know which ones are which?"

Pandora nodded, even though she honestly wasn't *exactly* sure.

"It's simple, then. You just have to make sure the box does not get into the hands of the evil ones."

"Well, it would be nice if I knew what the box does. Otherwise, it's going to be rather difficult to protect it."

"The box doesn't do anything. What needs to be protected is *inside* it. It is the contents that have the power whose misuse could plunge Mystic Notch into the deep abyss of an evil greater than mankind has ever known."

Pandora twitched her whiskers. That sounded a bit overly dramatic. Was the cat exaggerating?

Obsidian noticed her skeptical expression. "Trust me on this. The cats are in danger and, once the cats are gone, the way will be paved for evil to run rampant. You know how inadequate the humans are at protecting themselves." Obsidian paused for effect, then added, "My human was burned alive over it."

Hmmm. Okay, that sounded pretty drastic. Pandora was sure the other cats had not heard of this and the news made her feel important. She didn't want Mystic

Notch to be plunged into an evil abyss. She liked things just the way they were.

The female ghost swirled over and Obsidian strutted back behind her cloak. "Good luck, kid."

"Hey, where are you going? You didn't tell me wha—" Pandora started, but they were already gone, leaving Pandora staring at empty space.

"Pandora, what are you yowling at?" Willa asked.

Pandora blinked up at her. Dang, the ghost cat hadn't even told her what exactly was in the box or how someone might use it against them. All she knew was that Striker had the box. Her gaze flicked to the window where she could see Striker's cruiser pulling away from the curb. Did he have it in his car? At his house? She would have to use her superior detecting skills to figure where he was keeping it.

But if the contents were so dangerous, how would she get it safely into the hands of those that would protect it? And just exactly *whose* hands were those?

Pandora couldn't figure this all out on her own. Luckily, she knew where to get help.

CHAPTER 3

Pandora suffered through the rest of the day at the bookstore. She was anxious to bring the important information about the powerful box to the other cats, but she did not have an escape route at the bookstore like she did at home. The only way to get out of the shop was when Willa took out the trash, and she'd already done that.

So she passed the time by lounging in her cat bed and practicing patience.

Later that night, after obediently eating her supper and suffering through watching Willa and Striker make googly-eyes at each other over a large pepperoni pizza, she finally got her chance to escape.

Of course, she'd had to feign interest in getting into Willa's bedroom. It wasn't that she actually wanted to go in there and witness what Willa and Striker got up to in the dark. She had no interest whatsoever in that, but she'd discovered that whenever she insisted on being let into the room, it appeased Willa and made her less watchful. The more times she snuck in as Willa was closing the door, the less Willa would watch her later on.

So, whenever she wanted to escape, she made sure to pretend like getting into Willa's bedroom was the most important thing on her mind. That night, she'd snuck in and been turned out three times.

After they had closed the door for good, Pandora spent some time gazing into the crystal ball that sat on Willa's coffee table. This was an activity that Willa thought was 'amusing' but which Pandora knew was actually serious work.

The ball was a vital source of information, especially when it came to the mystical goings-on in Mystic Notch. Willa, however, always failed to see the mysterious things that were revealed in the crystal. She actually thought it was just a plain old paperweight.

Unfortunately, that night it was of no more use to Pandora than an old paperweight. No clues were revealed, and when the moon appeared halfway in the night sky, Pandora snuck out her secret exit in the basement and trotted over to visit the cats of Mystic Notch.

The cats took up residence in the barn of Willa's neighbor, Elspeth Whipple. Elspeth had been best friend to Pandora's first human, Anna, who was Willa's grandmother.

Pandora raced through the woods to the sound of owls hooting and peepers peeping. The warm, perfume-scented night air was still, but the speed at which she ran ruffled her fur and pushed her whiskers back. Even though she had excellent sight in the dark, the glow of the moon was a welcome beacon and revealed a myriad of nighttime animals, including some tasty looking chipmunks who scurried in the leaves. Pandora did not have time to chase them, though. She was in a hurry.

Thinking about Elspeth always made her think of Anna. Pandora's heart clenched. Anna and Pandora had been very close. Anna, like Elspeth, was in tune with the cats. Anna had been a joy to train and the two of them had had an easy rapport. She had almost gotten to the point where Anna would understand her telegraphed thoughts, just before the old woman passed. Pandora had inherited Willa shortly after. She'd come with Anna's house and the bookstore, so Pandora didn't have much choice. Unfortunately, Willa was not as quick a study as Anna and Pandora had little hope of training her to such a high level, even though she was becoming quite fond of her.

Pandora burst out of the woods, the red, two-story barn looming up in the clearing next to Elspeth's storybook gingerbread Victorian. The barn door was open a crack, just wide enough for her to squeeze in.

Inside the barn, the smell of hay and dry wood made her nose twitch. Oval, slitted eyes, in various shades of green, gold, orange and blue peered at Pandora from behind bales of hay, above in the hay loft and on top of stacked pallets. The barn hummed with unseen energy as the cats of Mystic Notch dialed up their senses and came forward to greet her.

"What brings you here?" the large, black cat, Inkspot, their leader, asked from his perch atop two stacked bales of hay.

Pandora puffed up. "I have important news."

The cats crept forward from their hiding places. Snowball's fluffy, white fur glowed in the small shaft of moonlight that spilled in from the open doorway. She assessed Pandora with curious eyes. "Important news about what?"

"Something's been unearthed. Something that could have evil consequences for the cats and people of Mystic Notch." Pandora had to admit that she was being purposely vague so as to draw out the moment. It wasn't often that she got to come to the cats with an important discovery.

"That's not necessarily news." Otis, the fat calico, sat on top of a stack of pallets and studied his perfectly honed shivs. "I already knew about it. Heard this morning from Ming."

Inkspot turned his green gaze on Otis. "Who is this Ming and why did you not bring an important discovery to the group?"

"I was doing the requisite legwork to determine if it really *was* important." Otis glared at Pandora. "Unlike some members, I do not bring every little thing to the group until I do the appropriate research."

The hairs on Pandora's back stood on end. It was just like Otis to try to steal her limelight and make it seem like she was over-reacting. He had been a thorn in her side since the very beginning. The cantankerous calico was one of the older cats, stuck in the old ways, who disapproved of the new methods Pandora liked to use.

Pandora wasn't sure if that was the only reason he had taken such a dislike to her, or if it was just in his obstinate nature to be contrary. He was always rubbing it in her face that being a male calico was extremely rare. Only a small percentage of calico's were male, and he seemed to think that made him 'special', whereas Pandora was just a common, mixed-breed shorthair.

But sometimes, underneath his air of superiority, Pandora could swear she sensed the teensiest flicker of humility, as if he wasn't really as stuck-up as he made out to be. This, however, was not one of those times.

She bristled at his comment about doing research. She had to admit she didn't have any hard research to back up her claim. She had something much better, though.

"I didn't need to do research. I was told about it by a ghost cat, so I know it is a true threat." Pandora shot Otis a smug look. She could see ghosts and he couldn't, a fact which she liked to rub in his face whenever she could.

"What ghost was this? Are they always truthful? I think some research would be prudent," Otis hissed.

"Stop the fighting," Inkspot growled. "Both of you tell me what you know. Pandora, you go first."

The other cats crept closer as Pandora told them about the cloaked ghost and the conversation she'd had with Obsidian. When she was done, Inkspot turn to Otis.

"And what does this Ming know about this?"

"Ming is very close to his human, Oscar Danforth. Apparently, there was a groundbreaking ceremony for the new historical society building where this box that Pandora speaks of was unearthed. Ming said his human was very upset about it. Ming sensed the box contained something very important which could be vital to our cause. That's why he mentioned it to me."

Kelley, the Maine Coon, swished her tail. It was enormously fluffy and when she swished it, everyone noticed. "So, what's so important about what's in the box? And where is it?"

All eyes turned to Pandora and her stomach did a nervous flip. She hadn't been able to get that information from Obsidian. Maybe she *should* have waited to bring this news to the group. "I don't know exactly what's in it, but it's something that can be used to harm us. Obsidian mentioned the two-faced cat in particular. And he said it was so important his human was burned to death for it."

The cats hissed. Some of them humped up their backs. The thought of being burned alive was not a pleasant one.

Everyone's eyes slid toward the back corner of the room where Hope, a young chimera with a half-black and half-orange face, sat calmly on top of a stack of wooden boxes. Hope was a cat with extreme magical ability, but she was too young to have honed it properly. The cats of Mystic Notch were protective of her, knowing that in the future she could be instrumental in helping them keep the balance of good. Pandora herself had bonded with Hope when they'd narrowly escaped death together earlier that year. Her heart squeezed at the thought of anything happening to the young cat.

"Very well. Then it seems that we should take this under consideration. We need to know more about what the box contains. You say that Striker has it?"

"I'm not exactly sure about that," Pandora said. "Obsidian said he had *access* to it, but I don't know where he is keeping it. I'm sure I can find out if I—"

Otis had padded into the middle of the circle of cats that had crowded around Pandora. He interrupted her, practically pushing her out of the way. "I know where it is."

"Where?" Snowball asked.

"Ming's human said it had been taken into police custody at the Mystic Notch police station. There is some question as to who it belongs to. Anyone who thinks it belongs to them must put in a claim with the appropriate paperwork to prove it. Ming's human is doing that now," Otis answered.

"Well, we certainly can't do that. We're just cats," Sasha, the Siamese, said.

"True," Otis nodded. "But we can influence our humans to do that. I think our best bet is to try to telepath our intentions to Elspeth. We already know she is sympathetic to the cats and on our previous attempts to communicate with her, we have had some limited success."

The other cats nodded and murmured their agreement.

Limited success? Pandora couldn't believe her ears. Were they actually considering relying on communicating with humans? Near as she could tell, the humans were slow on the uptake. That plan was fraught with all kinds of problems. Not to mention that it could take way too long and in the meantime, the box could fall into enemy hands ... like maybe this Oscar Danforth person.

"Hold it!" she cried out. "This is an urgent matter. Ming said his human is already preparing the paperwork to take it and we have no idea if we can trust *him* with it. We can't depend on the humans. We can figure out how to do this on our own." Her tail thudded sharply against the floor for emphasis.

Otis shook his head slowly, and in the most patronizing of manners. "Hold your horses, young one. It is true that we don't know if Ming's human is trustworthy. We do not want him to take possession. But I think we still have some time. I know that you favor the new ways, but sometimes the old ways are best."

Pandora's blood boiled. The old fart would wait so long that the whole town would be ruined. She didn't dare say that, though. The cats' society depended on respect and he was her elder. She turned to Inkspot.

"I don't think we have any time to waste. If it's at the police station, I think I know a way that we can get at it," she pleaded.

Inkspot tilted his head to consider her plea. "I am not totally against going in ourselves, but if the police are holding it until someone can make a case that they are the rightful owner, I think that means we have time. It should be safe at the police station. In the meantime, I think we should do our due diligence and research this box to uncover the real story. Only then will we know to whom we should entrust it."

"I object!" Pandora blurted out. "Nothing is safe when it comes to evil forces."

"I can't argue with that," Otis said in his annoying, passive-aggressive manner, "but the best way to handle this is through influencing the humans the old way. That is the only way the humans will think the outcome is of their doing."

"What say you all?" Inkspot asked.

The others exchanged glances, then one by one nodded their agreement.

Kelley looked at Pandora apologetically. "Only since we have time. It seems like the best way."

Pandora nodded and accepted the group decision. Maybe they were right and she was being too rash. But she didn't think so. No one else seemed to feel the same urgency that she did. Maybe it was because they had not talked to the ghost cat in person.

She took her leave. As she trotted away from the barn, a rock lodged in the pit of her stomach. Despite what the others thought, she knew getting possession of the box was critically urgent and if no one else wanted to take action now, she would just have to do it all by herself.

CHAPTER 4

The next day, Pandora awoke to the weight of her lonely task. She pretended as if nothing was different, though, because she didn't want Willa to get suspicious. She ate her Fancy Feast and obediently accompanied Willa to the bookstore in the Jeep. Once there, she settled down in the cat bed for her usual nap.

Except she didn't actually nap. She merely feigned sleep while waiting and watching for the moment when Willa would take the trash out to the dumpster. That was her only opportunity to escape the shop unseen.

It was risky, but she'd done it with success before. The secret was to slip out just as the door was about to close, and skulk low to the ground and close to the wall, then dart under the dumpster while Willa's attention was focused on wrestling the trash into the giant beast. Those other times Willa had never even missed her, thinking that she'd snuck off into the storeroom for a quiet nap as was her custom when the shop got busy. Later on, she could always sneak back in through the front door with the customer traffic. This method was more risky, though, so she chose to use the dumpster escape method whenever possible.

When she finally saw Willa struggling with the trash bag, she sprang into action. Forcing herself not to rush, she leisurely got up from the cat bed, yawned and trotted over to the storeroom door.

"Going into your private nap already?" Willa bent down and petted Pandora affectionately.

A pang of guilt stabbed Pandora. She hated deceiving her human. But she consoled herself in the knowledge that what she was doing was for Willa's own good as well as that of all the humans and cats in Mystic Notch.

Pandora trotted into the storeroom. Then, once Willa turned her back, she padded back to the doorway. Standing in the shadow of the cracked-open door so Willa would not notice her, she watched as Willa opened the back door and pulled the trash bag through, her attention focused on the small dumpster against the wall of the store five feet away.

Pandora snuck out just before the door closed, and hugged the wall, then squeezed under the dumpster, waiting until she heard the door slam, announcing that Willa was back inside.

The first part of her mission a success, Pandora crawled out from underneath the dumpster. She shook off the particles of paper and cardboard, then thanked the great cat goddess Bastet that the dumpster was not filled with garbage, before trotting off in the direction of the police station.

The police station was easy to get into. The doors were constantly being opened and Pandora had learned long ago that humans rarely look down at their feet. If she made herself small enough and skimmed close to the walls, she could go practically anywhere, almost as if she were invisible.

Once inside, she hunkered down under an orange plastic chair. The industrial tile floor was cold on her paws. The smell of sweat and paperwork permeated her nostrils and she dialed down her senses just a tad so as not to be overwhelmed by it while she considered her next move.

Where would they keep an important box?

Pandora realized the humans probably didn't know how important the box actually was. Even though, they must have sensed something about it because, according to Otis, they had taken it to the police station to hold until the rightful owner could be determined.

Would it be in the evidence room? No. Probably not. Though that would've made it easy since Pandora knew how to get in there.

Maybe Gus had it in her office? That was probably why the ghost had said the Striker had access to it. The ghost couldn't plead with Gus because Gus did not have the ability to see ghosts. But Gus and Striker worked very closely together. He would have access to whatever was at the Mystic Notch police station.

As if being summoned by her thoughts, Striker's size thirteen boots came thudding down the hall. Pandora decided to follow him.

As she slithered around the corner, her decision was rewarded. There was Gus, holding a silver box. It had to be the box she was looking for!

Gus was talking to a wizened old man whom Pandora did not recognize and a gnarled old woman whom Pandora knew was the head of the historical committee, Elizabeth Post.

"I don't know what the deal is with this box," Gus was saying. "But I'm not giving it to anyone until I'm satisfied they're the rightful owner. Not even the mayor."

The wizened old man wrinkled his brow. "The mayor? What does she have to do with this?"

"I don't see why it's any of your business, Danforth, but she called just this morning, trying to persuade me to give her the box."

"That's not right!" Elizabeth cried. "That box should be at the historical society."

"Rebecca thinks it still belongs to the town," Gus said.

"That's just stupid," Danforth said. "What's the town going to do with a silver box? Anyway, I have documented proof here that this belongs to my ancestor." Danforth shoved papers in Gus' face.

"Yes, you showed me those before," Gus said. "All they prove is that your ancestor knew about the box. It's just a diary entry with a drawing of a similar box."

"That's right. I never saw any evidence that your ancestor had this box in his possession. It was in the possession of Hester Warren. That's why it was buried in her yard. And that's why it belongs to the historical society." Elizabeth held her hand out toward the box, which Gus secured tightly against her rib cage.

"Well, if that's your argument, then Rebecca might be right because the town took Hester's land to pay for her trial," Gus said.

Elizabeth threw her hands up. "And what's the town going to do with it? Sell it? It's a valuable piece of Mystic Notch history and should be in the museum."

Danforth stepped closer to Elizabeth, drawing up to his full height of five foot five. "It's a valuable piece of my family's history and rightfully belongs to me."

Elizabeth stepped closer to Danforth so that their faces were now inches from each other. "It belongs to the historical society."

Striker pushed between them. "Hold it. No one is taking the box. We need to do some more research and look into legal precedents. And besides, Danforth, your paperwork doesn't prove anything."

Danforth glanced nervously at the box. "But what's inside it—it needs to be stored properly. If you guys drop that …"

His voice trailed off and everyone looked at the box. Gus held it out in front of her, her index finger sliding under the lip of the lid as if she were about to lift it. "Yeah, what exactly is this in here, anyway?"

Was Gus going to open the box? Curiosity overcame Pandora and she trotted out from her hiding spot as Gus lifted up the corner of the lid.

It was a fatal mistake. The movement caught Gus' attention and she glanced over at Pandora, her eyes growing wide. "What are *you* doing here?"

The lid snapped shut without revealing the contents.

Everyone turned to look at Pandora, who suddenly realized what the expression "deer caught in the headlights" actually feels like.

"Pandora?" Striker asked.

Pandora froze. She didn't know what to do. By the time she realized running was probably the best course of action, Striker had already lunged for her. For a human, he was very fast. He scooped her up in his arms before she had a chance to escape. She wiggled to get loose, but couldn't bring herself to sink her razor-sharp claws into him, so she was unable to escape his grip.

"If Willa finds you missing, she'll be worried sick. How did you get here?" Striker looked down at her with concerned, gray eyes.

"Mew." Pandora let out her most pathetic meow, hoping to get in his good graces.

It must have worked, because Striker laughed. "I'm going by the bookstore anyway. I'll just drop you there."

Across the room, Gus was frowning at her. "How does that cat get out so much? She seems to find her way to a lot of peculiar places where she shouldn't be."

Striker shrugged. "Cats are sneaky, aren't they?"

"I guess so." Gus tucked the box back under her arm and gestured to the door. "Now, if you people will all leave me alone, I have important police business to attend to."

"Fine," Elizabeth huffed. "But you haven't seen the last of me."

"That's right," Danforth added. "I may have to get my lawyer involved."

"Do whatever you think is necessary. I'm just following the town laws." Gus' fingernail made a metallic clicking sound as she tapped the top of the box. "In the meantime, I'm going to put this box in my office where no one can get it until I say so."

CHAPTER 5

The look of concern on Willa's face when Striker returned Pandora to the bookstore made Pandora feel like a heel. After a strict talking to, Willa cuddled her and then proceeded to shower her with her favorite chicken-flavored treats.

Pandora pretended to wiggle out of her arms during the cuddling, but the truth was she kind of enjoyed it—which made her feel even worse for worrying Willa. She couldn't explain to her human that she'd snuck out for the benefit of Willa and all of Mystic Notch.

Too bad she hadn't learned much at the police station. She didn't even get a look at what was in that darn box. Pandora padded around the bookstore, anxiously glancing in all the corners, hoping that Obsidian would appear to give her more information.

After a while, Willa became concerned about Pandora's strange behavior, and when she threatened a trip to the vet, Pandora settled into her comfy cat bed, arranging herself so as to get the most out of the slanting afternoon sun. She was almost asleep when the bell over the door jingled and the scent of lilacs and scones that Pandora associated with Willa's best friend, Pepper St. Onge, came wafting into the store.

Pepper owned a teashop down the street and often came in the afternoons with coffee or tea when business for both of them was slow. The two women liked to catch up over refreshments.

Pandora typically paid them no mind ... unless Pepper brought coffee because cream usually accompanied it, and if there was one thing Pandora loved, it was cream.

Pepper was dressed in a breezy, lilac skirt and lime green shirt with lace on the edges. She perched herself carefully on the edge of the purple micro-suede sofa that Willa had installed at the front of the bookstore for readers to lounge around on while they sampled the books.

Pandora watched through one slitted eye as Pepper slid the silver tray she'd brought down on the coffee table and starting unloading its freight— flowered cups, saucers, a pot, napkins, a dainty plate of scones.

The bitter smell of coffee hit Pandora's nose and her eyes came to rest on the silver creamer still on the tray. Suddenly she was very interested in joining the two humans as they snacked and gossiped. She rousted herself from her cat bed, stretched out her front legs and hopped down from the window.

"Hattie was in my shop buying some burdock root tea and she mentioned something about the goings-on at the groundbreaking ceremony this morning." Pepper expertly wrangled a waist-length strand of red hair back into the chignon at the nape of her neck and then poured dark coffee into two dainty, flowered cups. "What was up with that?"

"Rebecca plunged her golden shovel into the ground and almost ruined some antique box that was buried there," Willa said.

"A buried box? You mean like a treasure chest?"

"No, I don't think it had treasure in it." Willa sat down, accepted the coffee cup from Pepper and picked through the pile of scones until she found her favorite raspberry white chocolate flavor.

"What was in it? Hattie didn't say, but she said there was some kind of fight going on over it."

"Yes, there was. A few of the people in attendance seemed to think it belong to them. I didn't see what was in it, but the box looked all fancy."

The two women were ignoring Pandora. She walked by the edge of the coffee table, flicking her tail up over the top so that they would notice her. Didn't they know she was in need of some cream?

Willa pushed her tail away. "Shoo, Pandora. We don't want cat hair in our coffee."

Shoo? Pandora did not shoo. Instead, she jumped up on the chair where Willa sat and head butted her coffee cup, causing some of the liquid to splash out on Willa's gray tee-shirt.

"Geez, Pandora, I don't know what is with you today.

Lucky thing I'm not wearing any good clothes." Willa put down her cup and unceremoniously placed Pandora on the floor.

Pandora's golden-green eyes locked on Pepper's emerald ones. She tried to telegraph a message to her.

Put cream in saucer.

"Why? What's with Pandora?" Pepper's hand hovered over the creamer.

Pandora stared at her intently, her entire being focused on transmitting the message for Pepper to grab the creamer and pour some into a saucer.

"Somehow she got out today and Striker found her down at the police station." Willa blew out a breath, pushing the unruly copper curls away from her forehead. "Sometimes I don't know what I'm going to do with her."

"She always was adventurous." Pepper looked down at Pandora, and Pandora took the opportunity to intensify beaming her message.

Pour the cream into the saucer and place it on the floor.

Pepper frowned at her hands. Her cup was in her right hand poised halfway to her lips. The saucer rested in her left. Pandora watched with rapt attention as Pepper placed the cup on the coffee table and reached for the creamer.

Yes! Victory flooded through Pandora as Pepper poured a little bit of cream into the well in the middle of the saucer and put it on the floor. It seemed Pepper was not as dumb as she looked.

Pandora went to work on the saucer, first sniffing it

as if she suspected foul play, then hunkering down and sticking the very tip of her tongue in daintily. Forcing herself to go slowly—she had to keep up appearances and no cat wanted to appear too eager, even when it came to cream—she started lapping the thick liquid. It was like heaven. Ambrosia of the gods. She almost forgot to pay attention to the humans' conversation, which she would not have had the slightest interest in if they had not mentioned the curious box.

"Anyway, Gus has it at the police station because Elizabeth, Oscar and Rebecca were fighting over it. She said she would treat it like a found item and they would have to prove their ownership," Willa was saying.

Pepper's brow creased. "Why did they each think it belonged to them?"

"Elizabeth thought it should go to the Historical Society. Oscar said it was part of the Danforth family heritage."

"What about Rebecca? What would the mayor want with the box?"

"She said it belonged to the town because the town owns that land. They took it from Hester Warren back when she was burned as a witch."

Pepper picked up her cup and leaned back on the sofa, her top teeth worrying her bottom lip. "That's right. That land used to belong to Hester Warren. Doesn't it seem odd the town has owned it all this time and never done anything with it?"

"It does seem odd and it also seems odd that the one spot we chose to do the groundbreaking yielded this fancy box."

"*Very* odd." Pepper took a sip of coffee. "What was in it?"

"That's the thing, I never got to see that. And Striker never even looked! I asked Gus, but she was vague … you know how she can be."

"What did the box look like?"

"It was silver. I think it might have been sterling because it was very ornate with embossing around the edges and some sort of reptile in the middle."

Pepper leaned forward. "A reptile? Could it have been a newt?"

Willa nodded. "I suppose. Why? Do you know something about it?"

"Not really. It's just that Grandma St. Onge used to tell me this old family story. You know, the St. Onges have been in Mystic Notch for centuries, right?"

"Who hasn't?" Willa asked. Most of the town proudly boasted of their ancestral ties to Mystic Notch.

"Pretty much everyone, I guess. The St. Onges go back well past the 1600s. And my mother's side, too. So do the Posts. Riley Post married Bedelia Phipps in the late 1600s and started a whole other side of the family, including the Devons from whom Rebecca's father comes. Grandma St. Onge is the one I got all my herbal knowledge from. She was quite well known for it back in the day," Pepper said proudly.

Willa raised a skeptical eyebrow. Pepper fancied that her herbal teas had special properties. She claimed the right tea could have magical effects, not only on healing people but on other aspects of their lives, too. Willa wasn't sold on that, but Pandora knew that herbs did have special properties and she'd seen Pepper's tea work magic quite a few times.

"So what was the story?" Willa tapped her finger on the rim of her coffee cup.

"Oh, right. Well, she always made it sound like it was some kind of old family lore handed down over the generations. She said her grandma told it to her. But I kind of thought it was just a made-up story, like a fairy tale. The funny thing is she always mentioned a fancy silver box with a newt on it."

Willa shrugged. "Maybe that part was true. Your ancestors might have mixed real stuff with fiction to pass down a good story. One of the ancestral St. Onges might have known Hester and seen the box."

"They did know Hester. The town was small back then, so everyone knew everyone else," Pepper said. "Anyway, according to the story, the box is supposed to be some sort of sacred box that holds a vial of celestrium lily extract." Pepper looked at Willa very seriously over the rim of her cup. "According to St. Onge lore, the silvery blue liquid glows like moonlight and is very potent stuff."

Willa's brows tugged together. "That does sound like a fairy tale. I didn't see what was in the box. I guess it could have been a vial in there."

Pepper laughed. "Well, I doubt there is celestrium lily extract in it. In the world of herbs and energy, celestrium lily extract is supposedly very potent. It can amplify the potency of energy, healing stones and herbs to dangerous levels."

"What? That's just a mythical thing right? Like an old

wives' tale? I mean, I know *you* believe herbs and stones have energy, but if there really was such an extract, I'm sure you would be using it to pump up the volume on your tea."

Pepper shrugged. "Maybe. I doubt I would use it. It's too powerful. Anyway, the celestrium lily has been extinct for centuries. Grandma said there was no extract left."

"Right. It doesn't exist."

"But that doesn't mean it never *did* exist."

"Okay, I'll give you that, but that doesn't mean it's in the silver box we dug up."

Pepper's face turned grim. "I sure hope it wasn't in that box. Because a powerful extract like that could cause a lot of trouble if it fell into the wrong hands."

CHAPTER 6

Pepper's words echoed in Pandora's head. "... a powerful extract like that could cause a lot of trouble if it fell into the wrong hands."

The last drop of cream soured in her mouth as she turned away from the saucer. She knew Willa was taking Pepper's story with a grain of salt, but combined with the cloaked ghost, who Pandora now realized was Hester Warren, and what Obsidian had told her, Pandora was taking it a lot more seriously.

But whose hands were 'the wrong hands'? And was the extract even in the box?

She glanced around the store for any sign of the ghost cat. Willa always said human ghosts never came around when you *wanted* them to, and apparently it was the same for ghost cats. Pandora would have to figure it out on her own. Which was really no problem. She was smart.

While Otis and the Mystic Notch cats were spending time trying to persuade their humans to take action, Pandora would prove to them that her more modern ways were far superior. She would figure out who the bad guys were on her own.

But where to start? Pandora glanced up at Willa's computer. According to Willa, there were three parties who wanted the box. Oscar Danforth, Elizabeth Post and Rebecca Devon-Smyth. All Pandora needed to do was figure out which one had a motive to want to use the powerful extract. The computer was a good place to start, plus she could use the energy boost that being near the electronic device usually gave her.

Pandora knew how to surf the Internet without raising Willa's suspicions. She waited until Willa was busy stocking the shelves with new books. She couldn't see the computer from most of the aisles, so Pandora had free rein when Willa was out of sight. When Willa came back to the front or was fiddling on shelves within sight of the computer on the front counter, Pandora had to stop and pretend she was just sitting on the keyboard.

It was not the most efficient way to do research but Pandora couldn't let on that her seemingly random paw taps on the keys actually had meaning behind them.

Her efforts were rewarded. She discovered that the cloaked ghost was indeed Hester Warren and she'd had a cat named Obsidian. Hester was burned as a witch. There was no mention of the cat after that and Pandora felt glad the cat was not burned with her.

It was no surprise that Elizabeth Post and Rebecca Devon-Smyth had Mystic Notch family ties dating back to the 1600s. Most Mystic Notch residents' lineage went back even before that to when the town was settled. Willa's family went back that far, too. Willa had never traced it herself, but Pandora knew.

Perhaps the most surprising thing was discovered when Pandora looked into Oscar Danforth's lineage. It appeared one of his ancestors, Miles Danforth, was a town official in 1656 and he was the one who had accused Hester Warren of witchcraft.

Was he after the silver box? It was too much of a coincidence. Pandora's whiskers twitched. She was on to something.

Hester had known the box was important. She'd probably buried it to keep it out of the hands of the wrong people. Clearly, Miles Danforth was one of those people. Obsidian had guarded the box for as long as he could, but a cat can only live for so long … even if they do have nine lives. Obsidian was gone, the box unearthed and now it was up to the cats of Mystic Notch to continue protecting what was inside it.

This new information was critical, but what should she do with it? Pandora considered going it alone. Could she do something to stop Danforth on her own? She wanted to show the other cats, especially Otis, that her new methods worked, but there was too much at stake for her to take action based on her own ego. She would need more help so it was best to talk to the other cats and then come up with a plan of action based on this new evidence.

Pandora hunkered down on the keyboard and stared at the screen while she considered her options. The keyboard was warm and the energy radiated into her body, making her stronger. She closed her eyes just for a second …

"What are you doing? I hope you didn't inadvertently hit some buttons and send the email to Striker like you did last time." Willa was looming over her, a stern look on her face. Had she fallen asleep?

Pandora tried not to snicker. She'd sent that email on purpose when Willa and Striker were in one of their 'off-again' phases. It had been a bit awkward with Willa denying sending it and thinking Striker was making it up in order to see her, and Striker thinking it was weird Willa wouldn't admit to sending it, but the email had worked and the two of them had kissed and made up. Pandora puffed her fur up proudly. If only Willa knew the lengths Pandora went to for her human's happiness.

But instead of praising her, Willa scooped her off the keyboard and dumped her on the floor.

"Stay away from the computer." Willa frowned at the screen, which still displayed the article about Danforth's ancestor. "I didn't leave this up. It worries me sometimes what you do on here. I wouldn't put it past you to inadvertently order something expensive." Willa glanced at Pandora out of the corner of her eye.

Pandora considered that. She hadn't thought about ordering something online. Maybe she could put in an order of some of her favorite catnip while Willa wasn't looking.

She wouldn't be ordering anything today, though.

Disappointment washed over her as she watched Willa close down the computer. She'd had a slight hope that Willa might have caught on to what was going on with the box when she'd seen the article about Miles Danforth. It would be a lot easier if Willa figured out the real truth about Danforth, but, as Pandora already knew, humans didn't catch on that easily. She couldn't depend on Willa or any other human to protect what was in the box.

Pandora slunk over to her cat bed in the window. Now, more than ever, she needed to take action. It all made perfect sense. Danforth was trying to carry on the work of his ancestor. No wonder he was claiming the box was his. He wanted to get his hands on it for his own evil doing.

Even though the box was secure in Gus' office at the police station, Pandora felt that something needed to be done about him right away. She needed to talk to the other cats. But she didn't want to wait until Willa moseyed on home and went to sleep. She wanted to talk to them right away. Unfortunately, Willa had already taken the trash out, so Pandora wouldn't be able to sneak out the back door.

It was almost closing time and Pandora knew of one way that she could get to Elspeth's house and visit with the cats in the barn without having to wait until later that night.

She crouched down in her bed, narrowed her eyes and focused her entire being on telegraphing one thought to Willa.

Visit Elspeth.

CHAPTER 7

You know, I think I should visit Elspeth tonight," Willa said one hour later as she and Pandora trotted out to the Jeep. "I like to check in on her every couple of days and I haven't been in few. What do you say we go on over before supper?"

"Meow." Pandora nodded her head vigorously. Her intense hour of thought-beaming had finally worked! Maybe there was hope for Willa after all.

Pandora curled in a ball and tucked her face under her tail for the short ride to the old, white Victorian home that Willa had inherited from her grandmother. Elspeth lived a couple of streets over, but there was a path through the woods—the same path Pandora had taken the night before—that Willa took when she went to visit. Willa always let Pandora come along with her and, while Willa and Elspeth sat in the kitchen chatting,

Pandora usually took the opportunity to meet with the Mystic Notch cats in Elspeth's barn.

This night was no different. She trotted alongside obediently as Willa navigated the short path that ended at Elspeth's side yard. The old woman sat in a rocking chair on her porch as if she was expecting them. Pandora followed Willa up the steps of the mint green and pink gingerbread style house to the wide, wrap-around porch, deftly avoiding the thorny branches of the thick rose vines that grew all along the railing. The vines were lush with pink roses, releasing their perfumed scent into the air.

Tigger, the orange tomcat that guarded Elspeth religiously, was sitting beside her in the rocking chair. Pandora exchanged greetings with him while the two women exchanged their own greetings.

Elspeth bent down and scratched Pandora behind the ears, right where she liked it the most. "And how are you Pandora?"

Pandora rewarded her with a loud purr which made Elspeth laugh. "I guess she's doing okay."

"She's her usual head-strong self," Willa said and Pandora hoped she detected a note of fondness in the human's voice. "Though I am a bit worried. She's acting very anxious lately."

"No doubt," Elspeth gave Pandora a knowing glance. "There's been a lot going on what with that box being found at the groundbreaking and all."

The two women launched into a conversation about the mysterious box, giving Pandora the opportunity to trot off to the barn, followed by Tigger.

It was still daylight so Pandora could see everything inside the barn—the hay bales, wooden pallets and dust motes in the air. There were crude ladders up to the hay-loft, and at the far end of the barn was a row of stainless steel cat dishes which Elspeth took pains to keep full and clean. The smell of sweet hay, warm wood and salmon dinner Fancy Feast spiced the air.

Inkspot looked up from a bowl of cat food when Pandora entered. "Greetings, Pandora. Do you bring us some news?"

Pandora had to force herself not to blurt out her discoveries too quickly. She didn't want to seem over-eager. She slowly told them how she'd overheard the conversation between Pepper and Willa regarding the celestrium lily extract.

"What makes you think that this mythical extract is actually contained in the box?" Otis addressed her in his usual irritating manner.

"It makes perfect sense," Pandora said. "The ghost cat, Obsidian, told me there was something very important in that box. Something that we didn't want to fall into the wrong hands."

"She has a point," Snowball said. "But still, we do not know whose hands to keep it from."

"I think I might have that figured out, too." Pandora's fur puffed out with pride. More cats came out from behind the bales of hay. They sat in a circle with their tails curled around them while Pandora told them about her research on the Internet.

"That's preposterous!" Otis said. "You know you can't trust everything you read on the Internet."

Pandora bristled. "Well, of course not, but this was history. It has to be correct."

"Otis has a point," Inkspot said. "We can't make a judgment based on one article. All the people interested in the box had ancestors that were around in 1656."

"As does one of our most hated enemies, one who already claims to be a witch," Kelley chimed in.

"Felicity Bates," Snowball said as if they all didn't know who she meant.

Felicity Bates had ties back to the beginnings of Mystic Notch and she'd also married into one of the oldest, and richest, families in town. Rumor had it that she fancied herself to be a witch, although Pandora didn't think she was a very good one.

Willa had had run-ins with Felicity before and, based on the outcome, Pandora doubted Felicity's magic was very strong. Then again, that might be a reason why she would be interested in the box. Maybe she hoped the lily extract would increase her powers.

"But she's not one of the humans trying to get the box," Pandora pointed out.

"Not overtly," Inkspot said. "But maybe she has formed an alliance with one of the others, or maybe she's trying to get it in a different way that has yet to be revealed."

"Maybe …" Pandora considered it. They could be right, but she doubted this was the case. Pandora had a very strong feeling this had something to do with Danforth … or did she just *think* that because she was the one who had discovered the information about his ancestor?

"And let's not forget about Fluff," Snowball hissed.

Pandora had recently had a run-in with Fluff, one of Mystic Notch's most evil felines. Pandora had barely escaped and managed, with the help of Hope, to outsmart the white Persian who looked like an angel but was really a devil in disguise. It was not lost on her that Fluff had taken up with Felicity Bates, which was a big surprise to everyone since she'd previously acted like she hated cats.

"Have you been able to influence Elspeth or any of the other humans in this matter?" Pandora decided to attack it from another angle. If the other cats' 'old ways' weren't working, maybe they would be more inclined to act on the information she found with her 'new ways'.

"I heard Elspeth and Bing talking about the box, but they were using such vague terms I couldn't tell if they had a plan," Tigger said.

"That's why *we* need to come up with one," Pandora stated.

"A plan for what?" Inkspot was the voice of reason. "We don't even know if this lily extract *is* what is contained in the box."

"That's true," Otis agreed. "If it is not the extract the box contains but something less threatening, then, perhaps, we do not have to act so hastily."

Pandora hissed out a sharp, exasperated breath. What was with the cats? They were so slow-moving. "But Obsidian said whatever was in the box could plunge Mystic Notch into the deep abyss of an evil greater than mankind has ever known, so even if it isn't the extract, I think we still need to act quickly, before—"

"Obsidian said what *was* in there," Inkspot interrupted her. "That was in his time over three hundred years ago. We don't know what's happened to the box over time. It's best we find out what really does lie inside before we make any rash decision."

"Okay, I'll give you that. But we need to find out what's in there pretty quick, in case it is something bad." Pandora said.

Inkspot nodded. "I agree."

"Okay. Good. So how do you propose we do that?" Pandora asked.

"I know of only one way."

CHAPTER 8

Dusk was Pandora's favorite time of day, but she didn't have time to enjoy the elongated shadows of the trees, the mellowing color of the sun as it approached setting, or the cool temperatures as she raced through the woods that provided a shortcut between Elspeth's house and the police station.

She hoped their task would not take a long time. She wanted to get back before Willa ended her visit with Elspeth and found Pandora missing from the barn. Her human was already a little nervous about Pandora's odd behavior and she didn't need to add any fuel to the fire that would make Willa watch her any closer or, worse, take her on an unnecessary trip to the veterinarian.

Pandora could have stayed back, but she had been unable to resist. She knew curiosity killed the cat, but she was dying to find out what was inside that box.

When they reached the edge of the police station parking lot, Inkspot motioned for them to duck into a narrow alley between the police station and the pizza place. They hunkered down behind a dumpster that smelled of stale dough and rancid vegetables. Pandora dialed down her senses to keep from gagging.

"You know where the box is?" Inkspot asked Pandora.

"Gus said she was going to keep it in her office," Pandora answered.

Inkspot turned to the others—Kelley, Sasha, Snowball and, of course, Otis, who Pandora thought only came along because he didn't want her to be in on something that he wasn't.

"We don't want to be too conspicuous," Inkspot said. "So only two of us will go in. Me and Pandora. We will locate the box, look inside and then return."

"Maybe whatever is in the box is small enough that you can take it with you," Snowball suggested.

Inkspot tilted his head to the left. "I don't know if that would be a good idea. We could leave it on the porch for Elspeth. I wonder if she would know what it is."

"I don't think we should meddle in the business of humans!" Otis hissed. "Until we know exactly what is going on it might not be safe for us to take whatever is in there, especially if it is a vial of this mythical celestrium lily extract." Otis' yellow eyes slid over to Pandora.

Pandora ignored him. "If it is easy to carry then why not take it? We are in agreement that whatever's in there is dangerous and should be given to the right parties, right?"

"Yes, this is true. But dropping it on the porch for Elspeth is risky. She might not know what to do with it and it could cause problems for her if she has to explain to the other humans how she came to possess it. I think it is best that we get a handle on what is going on first, and then decide if we need to take such drastic intervention," Inkspot said.

The alley door to the police station opened and Pandora saw their chance to get inside. She didn't want to waste all night out there arguing with the cats.

"Here is our chance," she whispered. "Let's not sit around talking all night when we could be *doing*."

She ignored Otis' hiss of disapproval and rushed across the alley.

Pandora and Inkspot kept to the shadows, skulking along the alley to the doorway, where they slipped inside just as the door was closing. The police station buzzed with the hubbub of conversation, clacking of computer keys and ringing of phones. It stank with the sweat of fear and stale booze from the drunk and disorderly arrests that made up the bulk of Mystic Notch's crime. Pandora dialed down her senses another notch and pressed on.

They made their way down the hall, taking care to hide in the shadows of doorways and under the hard, orange plastic chairs that seemed to be everywhere. A pair of red stilettos came out of Gus' office and click-clacked down the hallway causing Pandora and Inkspot to dive under a small table.

Pandora could not see who it was without revealing their hiding spot, but once the person had passed, the hallway was empty. Now was their chance to get into Gus' office unseen.

They scurried out from under the table. Pandora was feeling pretty good about the success of their mission until they rounded the corner into Gus' office and found it crowded with humans who were engaged in some sort of argument.

Pandora froze when she saw that one of those humans was Oscar Danforth, the other was Felicity Bates. Pandora and Inkspot entered unnoticed and hunkered down under a gray metal folding chair. Inkspot motioned with his tail toward Gus' standard-issue green metal desk. On the corner sat the silver box.

Pandora's eyes flicked from Danforth to the box. Was he trying to edge his way closer?

"No one is getting the box!" Gus was saying.

"I'm not sure what you're talking about," Felicity rasped, her red hair flowing about her head as if it was possessed. "I just came to get the town clerk to notarize Fluff's pedigree papers. I heard about the box and wanted to stop by. I never said I wanted to take it … but I would be interested to see what's in it."

Pandora shuddered as she remembered her earlier run-in with the evil white cat. She peeked out from underneath the chair, her gut churning when she saw a white, fluffy tail twitching from underneath Felicity's arms.

Fluff had some magical power that drained Pandora's energy. She certainly didn't want that to happen now. She needed her energy to get away, not to mention that she somehow had to get to the box on the desk and open the lid without anyone seeing—a task that seemed impossible given all the people who were pressed into the small room.

Maybe they should leave and try again another time? But with both Danforth and Felicity here, there might not be another time. Luckily, the humans were too busy arguing to pay attention to much else.

"You don't need to see what's in it. And Danforth, those papers still don't prove a thing." Striker stood in between everyone else and the box as if he was protecting it. Was he? Pandora wondered, because Striker seemed to be spending an awful lot of time in *this* police station when he had his own police station in the next county.

She remembered how Hester's ghost had been pleading with him to protect the box. At the time, Pandora didn't think he was taking the plea seriously. He seemed more concerned with making sure Willa didn't notice that he was talking to spirits. Maybe he had given it more weight than Pandora had thought. Maybe he'd had another chat with Hester and was watching over the box, making sure it didn't get into the wrong hands. But did Striker even know whose hands were the wrong ones?

Pandora wondered if she should back off and let Striker handle it, as Otis had suggested. No. She couldn't trust that he would take it seriously enough.

The humans kept talking but Pandora ignored their noise and focused on the silver box. She *had* to get a peek in that box without being seen.

She signaled Inkspot and they inched their way closer. They darted from under the chair and slid underneath Gus' desk, keeping close to the back where they would be in the shadows.

Unfortunately, their movements caught the attention of Fluff. They watched in horror as his furry, white head stretched down from Felicity's arms. He peered at them with his eerie, orange eyes.

"Hiss!" Fluff's evil glare froze Pandora in her tracks.

"Meowl!" Inkspot lashed out at Fluff with his oversized paw.

"Merrrl!" Fluff scrambled out of Felicity's arms, leaping under the desk. Pandora panicked. Fluff's magic was strong. He could zap their energy in an instant and the whole mission would have been for nothing.

"I'll occupy his attention, you look in the box!" Inkspot darted out from underneath Gus' desk. He leaped up onto her bookcase, running along the edge and spilling half a dozen books out onto the floor. Fluff followed him, spilling even more books. The humans all turned in that direction, taking their eyes away from the box on the corner of the desk.

Pandora took advantage of the pandemonium to sneak up on the edge of the desk. She crept over to the silver box and lifted the lid just enough to see inside.

Nestled in dark purple velvet was a glass vial. The silver stopper was shaped like the head of a newt, its body and tail wrapped around the thin glass which held a thick, silvery blue liquid that shimmered like moonlight. Celestrium lily extract.

"You!" Pandora jerked her head toward the sound of Gus' voice just in time to see Gus reaching for her.

She pulled her paw back from the box. The lid snapped shut. She lurched away from Gus. Her back legs scrambled across the desk, spewing a stack of papers in the air. Gus stopped her pursuit of Pandora and grappled at the whirlwind of paper.

Pandora leaped onto the back of Gus' old, wooden chair with enough force to knock it over. On her way down with the chair, she locked eyes with Inkspot, who was busy trying to avoid Striker's grasp. Pandora jerked her chin toward the hall in a signal to make their escape.

Striker stumbled forward and knocked over a table. Gus was still busy trying to catch the flying paperwork. Felicity was on her knees, trying to fish Fluff out from under the kneehole in the desk, and Danforth was standing with his eyes wide open.

Pandora and Inkspot careened out of the office and down the hall, making a run for the side door. Luck was with them—a patrolman was coming in just as they turned the corner. They quickly darted out the door. Pandora almost crashed into the red stilettos, but darted left at the last second and then made a beeline for the woods with the other cats following.

***

Pandora's heart thudded against her ribs as she raced back to Elspeth's. Would Willa still be there or would she have already left, venturing home alone after Pandora did not answer her call? Pandora was in luck. A quick trip onto Elspeth's porch to listen at the screen door revealed that the two women were still talking inside.

Pandora took the opportunity to go into the barn and discuss the situation with the other cats.

"It does look like the extract is in there," Inkspot told the other cats in the barn. "Pandora saw it."

"So what should we do?" Kelley asked.

"We must protect Hope." Snowball cast her blue eyes towards the small cat who was lounging in the loft.

The black side of Hope's face was toward them, the orange side in the shadows giving her face a more equal appearance. She cast a brilliant, green eye on them. "I don't need protecting. My powers are strong, as you have already seen."

"We can't take the risk of anything happening to you," Inkspot said.

Pandora could see the fur on Hope's back ruffle. Hope had been upset that she couldn't be included in the trip to the police station, but the cats felt it was best that she stay hidden away, in case there was trouble.

"Speaking of which," Sasha said. "I think it's time you get back to your home."

Elspeth took care of most of the cats in the barn, but like Pandora, Hope had a loving forever home. Like most of the cats in Mystic Notch, she had a little escape route that allowed her to come out and gather in the barn. Naturally, she didn't want her human to know about it, so Hope needed to get back before her human came home from work. Due to her precious nature, the cats insisted that someone accompany her for her own protection. Tonight it was Sasha's turn.

"Not yet," Hope said. "I want to hear the plan first."

"It seems obvious what we must do," Pandora said. "We know the powerful lily extract is in the box and we know that Danforth is after it. He was in Gus' office just tonight."

"And so was Felicity," Inkspot added.

"Of course. The two of them are probably in on it together!" Pandora paced around the room. "I don't think we have any time to waste. We need to take Danforth out of commission now."

"Wait a minute!" Otis objected. "We can't just go taking humans *out of commission* without ironclad proof."

He had a point. It was an unspoken rule that they didn't mess around in the business of the humans unless they had a really good reason.

"But we *have* proof," Pandora insisted.

"Pffft," Otis hissed. "That is not proof. Let me talk to Ming. He would know what his human is up to. I don't think Danforth is the one to worry about. Ming would have warned me if he was."

Pandora narrowed her eyes at Otis. "How do you know you can trust Ming? He could be in on it with them and acting like he's a friend. A spy, taking you into his confidence so he can get information on us from you."

"I don't like what you are insinuating," Otis huffed. "I've been friends with Ming for several of our lives and I'm wise enough to tell which side someone is on … don't forget, I have much more experience than younger cats such as yourself, and with experience comes finely honed senses."

"Or old, faltering ones," Pandora shot back.

"Stop fighting," Inkspot said. "I side with Otis. We don't want to go off half-clawed. Danforth's presence is circumstantial. You also saw Elizabeth Post there and Felicity. The truth is we don't know *who* is after the extract."

Pandora sighed in frustration. Why were the cats being so overly cautious? She was starting to think that they were getting lazy in their old age. Was she the only one that wanted to take quick action to prevent evil from destroying their town? "But Danforth's ancestor goes back to the time of Hester Warren. He accused her of being a witch. I saw it online."

"Most people in Mystic Notch have ancestors that go back that far," Kelley pointed out.

"But not all of them accused Hester of being a witch. I think Miles Danforth did that to get at the potion and that's why Hester hid it." Pandora could practically spit.

Inkspot shot her a sympathetic look. "I sense your frustration, but we cannot take action against humans until we are certain the threat is dire and the human we target is the right one."

"But Obsidian, the ghost cat, told me the threat *was* dire. His exact words were that this liquid could 'plunge Mystic Notch into the deep abyss of an evil greater than mankind has ever known'. And he alluded to Hope being a target." Pandora looked at Hope out of the corner of her eye. The young cat did not seem the least bit afraid and Pandora felt a rush of pride in knowing her. She was powerful and brave, and Pandora was honored that they were friends.

Otis padded forward until his face was mere inches

from Pandora's. "Well, if this ghost cat knows so much about it, then maybe *he* can tell you exactly who it is that we should *take out of commission*."

CHAPTER 9

Otis' words hung like a dark cloud over Pandora's heart as she snuggled into her cat bed at the bookstore the next morning. She wished she *could* ask Obsidian who the evil one was, but the ghost cat had not shown himself since that first day. Pandora didn't know what to do. She couldn't do much about Danforth on her own, and the box did seem to be safe at the police station, so maybe she should do as Otis and the others suggested and just wait. Too bad waiting was not her strong suit.

The click-clacking of high heels on pavement caught her attention and she looked out the window to see the same red stilettos she'd seen in the police station the night before. But this time, she could see who the owner was—Rebecca Devon-Smyth.

Had Rebecca been at the police station last night?

Pandora's face contorted as if she'd eaten a lemon. She didn't like Rebecca and, judging by the conversation that was coming from the purple micro-suede sofa, neither did the bookstore regulars.

"I don't think her outfits are very professional at all." Hattie twisted around to look out the window at Rebecca who sashayed across the street in a tight, red top and floral skirt that ended just above the knee.

"Certainly not for mayor of our town," Cordelia agreed. "And where is she going, anyway?"

"It looks like she's headed toward the First Hope Church," Josiah Barrows, the retired town postmaster said.

Cordelia snorted. "Church! I never saw her go there before."

"Probably trying to jazz up her image before the elections next year." Bing's white brows knitted together as he watched Rebecca disappear down the side street across from the library.

"I heard the Bates family made a big contribution to her campaign." Hattie twisted to face forward again.

Pandora's ears perked up at the mention of the Bates family. She hadn't realized they had a connection with Rebecca. She remembered that Felicity had been in the police station last night, too. Were the two of them combining forces to get the box? And if so, where did Danforth fit in?

Pandora made a mental note to do more research on the computer. She knew Felicity was not on the side of good, but near as she could tell, she didn't have ties to the box like Danforth did. Nor did Rebecca. Then again, maybe she hadn't researched far enough. Pandora had looked up Devon and Smyth and not found anyone … perhaps she hadn't traced the maternal lineage back enough. Her ancestor could be someone with a different last name.

Pandora's spirits sank. If the three of them were in on it together and they had Fluff on their side, the situation was grim. She glanced at Willa out of the corner of her eye. Maybe it was time to start ramping up the communications with her human, or maybe she should focus on Striker.

Striker seemed like a better bet. He had talked to Hester's ghost and his frequent presence at the police station indicated he may be there because of the box.

As if conjured by thoughts of the police, the door whooshed open and Gus stormed inside in her usual brisk, confrontational manner.

The regulars all raised their brows as Gus turned a stern face toward them.

"Morning, Gus. How are you?" Bing asked.

"Good." Gus nodded to them. "What are the rumors on the grapevine this morning?"

The regulars exchanged a look and shrugged.

"Nothing, really," Hattie said.

Willa narrowed her eyes at her sister. "What brings you here, Gus? A social visit? Or do you want something?"

Pandora figured it was the latter. Gus never stopped by for a social visit.

"We had a bit of a fracas down at the station last night and I was hoping there might be some scuttlebutt around town. Maybe one of you might have heard something." She slid her eyes over to Pandora who shrunk back in her bed. "I think I might have recognized someone there."

Willa turned to look at Pandora. "Pandora? She wasn't there. She was at Elspeth's with me last night."

Gus' left brow quirked up. "Uh huh. Funny, there was a cat that looked just like her at the station."

Pandora pasted her 'innocent' face on. Then she did the trick that always diverts suspicion and makes humans go 'awww'—she cocked her head to one side and rotated her ears forward then raised up her eyebrows just slightly so her eyes would look bigger.

"Inside the police station?" Hattie asked. "I didn't know you allowed cats in there."

"We don't," Gus said. "Not usually. But for some reason, there was a gaggle of them. Felicity Bates brought that white thing in and then some other cats apparently snuck in."

"Felicity Bates?" Bing's face was etched with concern. "What was she doing there?"

"Getting some papers notarized, or so she said." Gus crossed her arms over her chest. "Anyway someone stole the contents of the box that was dug up at the groundbreaking for the historical society sometime that night." Gus glared at Pandora as if she suspected her. "And I was wondering if any of your cronies had heard anything."

"You mean something was stolen from the police station?" Willa's lips quivered at the corners as if she was trying not to laugh.

Gus' face turned pink. "Yes. From my office."

"They didn't take the whole box? Just the vial inside?" Bing's face was serious.

Gus nodded. "I don't know why someone would want that so bad, but I do know three people who were trying to get their hands on the box, and two of them were there last night. Now, have any of you heard anything about it?"

The door whipped open before anyone could answer and Elizabeth Post stormed in. She stood in front of Gus, her hands fisted on her hips. "I heard the vial was stolen right out from under your nose. I demand you give me what's left before the rest of it gets stolen and is lost to Mystic Notch forever."

Gus narrowed her eyes at Elizabeth. "And how did you hear that so soon?"

"I have my ways. That box is an important piece of Mystic Notch history and it will be safe in the museum," Elizabeth said. "Apparently, a lot safer than in the police station, anyway."

"Sorry, no dice. I'm keeping the box until someone can make a valid claim or the time expires as per the law." Gus gave the group one last look as if giving them a final chance to enlighten her. No one said a word.

The concerned look on Bing's face made Pandora's heart twist. She knew Bing was one of the humans that tried to keep undesirable forces from gaining power in Mystic Notch. She should have listened to her instincts last night and taken the vial, then given it to Bing or Elspeth. She'd let the other cats overrule her intuition and now the celestruim lily extract was in the hands of the bad guys. She would not make that mistake again.

"Well, I never." Elizabeth's knees popped as she turned toward the group on the couch. "Don't you people think that box should be in the museum? It clearly belonged to one of our most interesting residents—Hester Warren."

"Indeed," Bing said. "It is a fine piece with a lot of history. You seem to be going to awfully great lengths to secure it."

Elizabeth scowled at him. "Well, of course I am. It's my job. Naturally I would be going to great lengths. I want to display it front and center. The question is why would Oscar Danforth and Rebecca Devon-Smyth be going to those same lengths? They don't have a museum to display it in, and I can't imagine why it would be so important to them. And if they wanted it, why not take the whole box?"

"Good question," Cordelia said.

"It doesn't make sense," Elizabeth continued. "I mean, *who* would steal that lovely vial and just *what* do they plan to do with it?"

CHAPTER 10

Pandora fidgeted in her cat bed. Now that someone had stolen the lily extract, it was only a matter of time before they used it. But what would they use it *for*? According to what little information Pandora had, the extract would amplify energy. Things like herbs and crystals could be made more powerful. Could it be used for other types of energy, too?

What exactly were Obsidian and Hester afraid would happen if it fell into the wrong hands? If only she had some clue, she could come up with a plan of action, but she had no idea where this person might strike and, therefore, no idea how to head them off at the pass.

A dark cloud of loneliness descended on Pandora. She couldn't depend on the Mystic Notch cats to help. They were clearly determined to proceed with an over-abundance of caution. She didn't want to waste time pleading with them again when the results would probably be the same.

Now that the vial had been stolen, that upped the ante. Pandora felt a sense of desperation. She had to do something fast.

But she couldn't go back to the cats in Elspeth's barn with the way they were acting, especially the obnoxious Otis. Saving Mystic Notch was all on her.

She trotted over to the sisal scratching post Willa kept next to the desk, to sharpen her claws while she thought about what to do next. She would have preferred to use the back of the sofa for sharpening, but the one time she'd done that Willa had become incredibly angry. She'd never done it again, even though the sofa called to her at these times when she wanted her shivs to be as sharp as razors.

Pandora had to admit the other cats did have a point. Her evidence against Danforth was compelling but wasn't proof of anything. She eyed the computer on the counter. She *should* research the other suspects and see if they had ties to Hester Warren, but Willa was hunched over the computer so Pandora wouldn't be able to access it until later. She didn't have time to wait for 'later'.

With limited time, Pandora figured her best bet was to check out the prime suspect, Danforth. Maybe she could catch him with the vial and take it from him before he did his dastardly deed. And if Danforth wasn't the one, at least she would have done *something*.

Pandora's eyes drifted to the full trash barrel. The regulars had left and Pandora knew Willa would soon be taking it out to the dumpster. She would have to be ready to make her exit. Pandora stopped working her claws and padded over to Willa, snaking around her ankles so that she would be noticed, then flicked her tail and headed toward the storage room. She glanced back over her shoulder halfway there to make sure Willa was watching.

Willa watched Pandora, then bent to pick up the trash. On her way to the back door, she poked her head into the storeroom where Pandora had already curled up in between two stacks of boxes and was pretending to sleep.

"That *wasn't* you at the police station, was it?" Willa frowned at Pandora who blinked at her innocently. "No. It couldn't have been. I saw you in Elspeth's barn. Gus just *thought* it was you."

Willa turned with the trash in her hand and Pandora silently snuck up behind her, slipping out through the open door. While Willa was focused on throwing the trash in the dumpster, Pandora slithered underneath it. She crouched down and looked around, her heart jerking in her chest when her eyes met another set of feline peepers blinking at her from the dark shadows of the corner.

"I've been waiting for you," Hope said.

"What are you *doing* here?" Pandora asked.

"I came to help you. I can feel the urgency in making sure the vial doesn't get into the wrong hands. I think the other cats are acting too slowly and, while I know the older ones have much wisdom, I think us younger cats have a lot to offer, too."

Pandora studied Hope's face. The dual colors were a

little unnerving. The coloring was split down the middle of her nose. One side was all black with a green eye, the other side was orange tiger-striped with a blue eye. It took a little getting used to.

Should she take her up on it? Like Pandora, Hope was a young cat in terms of lives lived. The two of them had forged a bond earlier in the summer when they'd gone up against Fluff and narrowly escaped a dire situation. Hope was powerful, but she was very important to their cause and if harm came to her, it could be devastating. Pandora shuddered to think of how much trouble she would be in with the other cats of Mystic Notch if harm came to Hope because of her … but she *could* use the help.

And if they didn't do something now, there might not be any cats—or humans—left in Mystic Notch to care.

"Okay, what do you think we should do?" Pandora asked.

"We must figure out who the evil one is. Have you gleaned any more information from the ghost cat?"

Pandora's hopes fell. She had not seen Obsidian since that first day, even though she'd focused many times on manifesting him. His advice would have been very valuable right now. "Sadly, I have not."

"Okay, then we are on our own. It sounds like there are three suspects. I agree with the others that we can't go off half-clawed and just attack one of them without provocation. But I also think it would take too long to depend on the humans to resolve this. So we need to eliminate the suspects and the best way I know to do that is to spy on them," Hope ventured.

Pandora nodded. That had been exactly her plan. The two were in sync. "Okay, but we must be careful. I found out disturbing news that makes our mission even more critical."

Hope's whiskers twitched. "What is that?

"I've discovered that the vial of celestrium lily extract we saw in the police station last night has been stolen."

"No!" Hope hissed. "So, the evil ones must intend to use it quickly."

"No doubt. Unless we can stop them."

"It seems like we have no choice."

"I'm afraid you are right." Pandora peeked out from under the dumpster to make sure the coast was clear, then shimmied out with her stomach low to the ground.

Hope followed, glancing around uncertainly. "Maybe this job is too big for the two of us. Should we tell the others?"

Hope had a point. Pandora didn't want to endanger Hope, but she also wasn't going to wait around for the others to make a decision. The least they could do was scout things out. Maybe they would get lucky and, if they were cautious, they would not come to harm. "We will tell the others, but in the meantime maybe we can do some surveillance. If we can bring them solid proof of *who* stole the extract, then perhaps they will agree to join with us to rid Mystic Notch of the one who would do us harm."

"Good plan. I think I know where we should start."

CHAPTER 11

Elizabeth Post lived on Vine Street and Hope new exactly which house. They trotted across town, belly-crawling under shrubberies and sticking to wooded areas so as not to be seen. It didn't take long before they were crouched at the edge of the woods overlooking Elizabeth's back yard.

The old woman was bent down, digging in the ground.

Pandora's whiskers tingled. "Is she burying something?"

Hope craned her neck for a better look. "She *is* digging in the dirt, but I don't think she is burying the vial. It looks like she's planting flowers."

Pandora's whiskers drooped in disappointment. Hope was right. Sitting next to Elizabeth was a flat of colorful pansies. Her gnarled hands stabbed at the dirt with a spade. She shifted her weight, her knees creaking and spasms of pain etched on her face. Still, she hummed as she worked.

Pandora had a sinking sensation that Elizabeth was not the one.

"She's just gardening. Wouldn't she be putting her evil plans into action if she was the person who stole the vial?" Hope's words reflected Pandora's thoughts.

"Yes, it does seem odd. Maybe she is putting on a front?"

Hope looked around. "For who? There is no one here but us."

"She's not doing anything even remotely evil," Pandora said. "I can't help but feel she is not the one."

"Maybe we should look in on the other suspects. I believe they were higher up on the list anyway, right?"

"Yes. I saw Rebecca heading toward the church earlier. Maybe we can catch her down there."

"The church? That is supposed to be a place of good," Hope said.

"I know." Pandora turned back toward the woods. "Maybe that makes it the perfect place to start a campaign of evil."

"What about Fluff?" Hope asked as they raced through the woods back to town. "He was at the police station with Felicity last night. I bet he is in on it."

"Oh, I'm sure Fluff is in on it. Or at least he wants to be, but I don't think Felicity's magic is up to par and she isn't the sharpest pencil in the box, so if she is involved, she must be working with someone else."

"And she was at the police station with Danforth last night."

"Exactly. And I think I saw Rebecca going out as we were going in."

"But you saw the vial in there *after* Rebecca left, so she couldn't have been the one who took it."

Good point. *They* were going on the assumption that someone had stolen the vial during the fiasco created by the cats. It made sense that Fluff started that whole thing specifically for that reason, so now they were back to Felicity ... and Danforth.

Pandora was familiar with all the paths in the woods, having traveled them her whole life. She took one that would dump them out behind the library, which was across from the street that led to the church, the same street she'd seen Rebecca walking down earlier.

As they crouched in the bushes next to the library, Pandora saw a familiar figure come out of that street.

"It's Danforth!"

"What is he doing?" The cats watched Danforth walking up the street away from the church, looking over his shoulder as if he expected someone to come up behind him ... or as if he was making sure no one saw him.

"Let's follow him!"

They scuttled out from underneath the bush, glanced up and down Main Street to make sure the coast was clear and then ran across.

Danforth had turned down a side street and Pandora and Hope whipped around the corner at high speed.

"What the—"

Pandora screeched to a halt seconds before her head slammed into an open car door. Not any car, though, a police car. Striker's police car.

"Pandora?"

Pandora stood frozen on the side of the road. What was Striker doing here? By the way he was sitting slouched down in the front seat of his police car, it almost looked as if he was engaged in some sort of surveillance. Did he harbor the same suspicions as she?

Striker turned his gaze to Hope. "And you. I recognize you, too. You guys shouldn't be out here. It's dangerous."

In a second, Striker was out of the car and reaching down to pick them up.

Pandora's heart fluttered with indecision. Should she run or let Striker capture them and put them in his car? A quick peek into his car gave her the answer. Sitting in the front passenger seat were the ghosts of Hester and Obsidian.

Pandora let herself be caught and Striker tossed her and Hope into the back seat, shut the door and then got into the driver's seat. He twisted around to look at Pandora.

"I don't know how you keep getting out of the bookstore, but Willa is not going to be happy." His gaze flicked to Hope. "And you … how did you get down here, anyway? I happen to know you live on the other side of town and are not supposed to be out."

Both cats blinked at him innocently.

"And don't try to get away by coughing up a hairball

in the backseat like you did last time." Striker pointed to a small plastic tube on his dashboard. "I picked up some hairball remedy, and if I see any sign, I will not hesitate to give you a good dose."

Pandora blanched at the thought of being forced to ingest the oily goop, but she couldn't help but smile to herself as she remembered how she'd escaped the car earlier in the summer by conjuring up a large hairball. She'd made an exaggerated show of gagging, belching and heaving, along with retching noises loud enough to wake the dead. All the commotion had caused Striker to stop the car and open the back door and what he saw on the floor mat had occupied his attention long enough for her to escape.

"Forget about the cats," Hester said. "Why don't you follow Danforth. I told you how Miles Danforth and Nathaniel Phipps were the ones who grabbed me and then fixed the trial. They were after the box back then and his relative is probably after it now."

Striker turned his attention to the insistent ghost.

"I told you. I'm not sure he *is* the one. I looked up the history like you suggested, but that still doesn't mean anything. That was over three hundred years ago. It's not like Oscar has been communicating with Miles about this." Striker frowned. "Unless he can talk to ghosts, too."

"But he's acting so suspicious." Hester wrung her ghostly hands together

"Lots of people act suspicious," Striker said. "Anyway, I need more proof before I can do anything. I can't just pick him up off the street for no reason. And I can't spend all my day on this, either. Maybe now would be a good time for you to run off and do whatever it is that ghosts do."

Pandora couldn't believe her ears. Striker was acting just like the Mystic Notch cats. He was ignoring what was right in front of him and claiming he needed more proof even though Hester, herself, had told him she suspected Oscar Danforth. What was up with everyone?

Obsidian looked around the front seat headrest at them.

"I see you have a friend working with you," he said to Pandora.

Pandora glanced over at Hope. Could she see ghosts? Judging by the confused way she was looking at Striker as he talked to thin air, she could not.

"Yes. We've teamed up to try to stop the evil forces from using the lily extract," Pandora said. "Did you know it was stolen?"

Obsidian's face turned grim. "I know. My human, or should I say ghost, knows as well. She has tried to convey the urgency of the situation to Striker, here, but he's a real stick in the mud. Seems unwilling to do anything without proof."

"Yeah, I know how that feels," Pandora said, thinking of the Mystic Notch cats and their demand for proof.

"Have you discovered anything that could help?" Obsidian asked.

"We have some suspects but we don't know which one to target. Nor what to do with them once we figure out who it is." Pandora flicked her eyes to the street where she'd last seen Danforth, but it was empty. He was long gone.

Striker started the car and reversed out onto Main Street. Pandora knew she only had a few minutes left of freedom before Striker returned her to the bookstore. She cringed, thinking of the restrictions Willa would inflict on her for this latest escape.

"We don't have much time to communicate," Obsidian said as Striker pulled up to the curb outside the bookstore. "Our strength here is getting weaker."

Pandora could see their ghostly figures were barely discernible now, but she wasn't too nervous at the thought of losing Obsidian's counsel—he hadn't really been around to help her much, anyway. "Is there anything you can tell me that would help? Something you might know from your vantage point of the spiritual plane?" Pandora asked as Striker came around to her door.

"Unfortunately, the spiritual plane isn't all it's cracked up to be." Obsidian's ears twitched. "We barely get any information over here. But I do have one word of advice."

Striker opened the car door and reached toward Pandora. She spread all four of her legs out wide so as to stop him from pulling her out of the car just long enough so she could hear Obsidian's advice.

"Well, what is it?" she hissed.

"You must be suspicious of old alliances—the evil forces of the ancestors could be at work through their descendants. As you know, the old ways are strong. You have everything you need to know inside you. Trust the old ways … and, as you modern souls say, go with your gut, kid."

Pandora relaxed her legs and Striker pulled her out, tucked her under his left arm and grabbed Hope with his right.

Pandora craned her neck to look at Obsidian. "Go with my gut? What the heck is that supposed to mean?"

Striker was already striding toward the door with Pandora and Hope securely held. Pandora looked over Striker's shoulder at the police car, but Obsidian had already turned away. So much for Otis' suggestion that Obsidian might know whom they should target. He didn't know squat. And what was worse, his advice stunk. He'd only given her the vague instruction to trust to old ways and go with her gut. Now she'd have to figure out exactly what he'd meant by that.

CHAPTER 12

As it turned out, Pandora had plenty of time to reflect on the meaning of Obsidian's words. She realized it was some kind of obscure message. Why couldn't ghosts just come out and say what they meant? They were always so flighty.

She let his words drift through her mind, trying to dissect each sentence and find the hidden meaning. He'd mentioned the old ways were powerful. Did he mean that she should pay more attention to the older cats in the barn?

But he'd also said to go with her gut *and* that the evil forces of the ancestors could be at work through their descendants. She already knew Danforth's ancestor was one of the men who had accused Hester. Then again, almost everyone involved had ancestors dating back to

Hester's time. But her *gut* told her the Danforth was up to something.

Maybe now, given that the vial had been stolen, the other cats would see things her way. Obsidian's message about the old ways being powerful could have meant for her to give the cats another chance before she acted on her own. Either way, she would have to wait until later that night since she was now trapped in the bookstore.

Willa had been shocked when Striker had dropped her and Hope off. She'd immediately shut the store room door—mistakenly thinking that's where Pandora had escaped from—and made sure all exits were secured.

Pandora had had to endure a stern talking to, throughout which she'd feigned indifference, then Willa had called Hope's human, leaving a message because the human was at work.

With all exits blocked and Willa casting a periodic watchful eye on them, Pandora and Hope were left with no choice but to snuggle into cat beds in the window and take much-needed naps. Which was exactly where they were later that afternoon when Elspeth rushed into the store surrounded by waves of turbulent energy. Pandora sensed the worry in the older woman and turned up her senses. Something was terribly wrong.

Willa must have sensed it, too. Her brow creased as she addressed Elspeth. "What's wrong?"

Elspeth glanced down at the cat beds, her eyes widening when she noticed Hope. "Thank goodness the two cats are safe."

"What?" Willa's face wrinkled into a puzzled look.

"I'm sorry. I'm just a bit frazzled." Elspeth patted the

wisps of snow white hair that had escaped from the thick bun on top of her head. She glanced around the shop to make sure no one else was there, then whispered, "I've just come from the feral cat station by the church and I'm afraid I have some terrible news."

"What is it?"

"It seems some of the feral cats have been poisoned." Elspeth's voice cracked as she said the words.

Pandora's heart twisted. The feral cats poisoned? She ached for her fellow felines, even though she was only acquainted with a few of them.

Willa gasped. "No! How many cats? Are they dead?"

Elspeth shook her head. "Seven of the cats were affected. Thankfully, they are not dead, but Doc Everett doesn't know if he can save them."

"It must have been someone from town who doesn't like the cats. They must have figured out we were sheltering them in the building on the church grounds this month," Willa said. "But poisoning them is going too far."

Elspeth glanced over at Pandora and Hope. "Yes, much too far …"

"What did they poison them with? I know the cats are always very suspicious of strangers and cautious of what they eat. Did they spike some food they couldn't resist?"

Elspeth's eyes were still locked on Pandora's. "Something like that. It seems they were given some sort of catnip. It was laced with something that made it very strong. The cats are very ill, in a catatonic state just like if you overdosed on a medicine."

"That's terrible. Pandora escaped earlier and I'm just very grateful that Striker found her and brought her back. I don't know what I would do if she were poisoned." Willa glanced over at Pandora and Pandora's heart melted at the human's concern for her. Willa really did care. Which made it all that much more important for Pandora to ensure Danforth was stopped before he could do any more harm.

"It goes without saying that I'm very concerned about the cats. This doesn't bode well." Elspeth snuck another look at Pandora.

Was the old lady trying to tell her something?

Pandora let the humans chatter on. She turned to Hope. "Do you think this has something to do with the vial."

Hope looked out the window, only the dark side of her face visible to Pandora. "It sure sounds that way. The celestrium lily extract would amplify the potency of the catnip. It would be just as Elspeth has described. The cats would literally overdose on the herb."

"But why would Danforth want to kill the feral cats? They do not have the magic like we do," Pandora pointed out.

Hope turned to face Pandora full on and Pandora was stricken by the startling contrast of her friend's split-colored face. "I think he was just practicing, experimenting to find how much of the extract he needed to use in order for it to be fatal. And then, once he has the amount perfected, he plans to use it on us."

Pandora's stomach clenched in fear for Hope. The two of them had almost died together and had fought their way out side by side. She felt fiercely protective of the younger cat, like a big sister.

Pandora didn't want to fall into the clutches of Danforth, but of all the cats, Hope must be protected the most. The old scrolls had shown she was the one with the most power and Pandora knew the balance of that power had yet to develop. If the evil-doers wanted to put a wrench in the works for those on the side of good, killing Hope was the way to do it.

Pandora's words were grim, "And now that they've practiced and seen the outcome, there isn't much time left to stop them before they put it to the intended use."

CHAPTER 13

Pandora felt a huge sense of relief when Elspeth volunteered to take Hope back to her forever home. Elspeth was on the side of good and she would make sure the young cat was safe. Even though her heart tugged when Elspeth took Hope away, she knew it was for the best.

As the day wore on, anxiety built in Pandora until she was coiled like a spring. She wanted desperately to be taking action, but had no choice other than to sit in her cat bed in the window. Willa had already taken out the trash and it was a slow day, with no customers opening the door for her to attempt an escape.

On the upside, it gave her a lot of time to think about trusting her gut. She'd felt Danforth was the culprit all along and with what she'd discovered on the internet and what Hester had said to Striker, she had convinced herself that he was the one.

Okay, she had to admit, she had a niggle of doubt because Striker had doubt, and she trusted his instincts. But something had to be done and stopping Danforth seemed like the best course. She only hoped that this terrible news would spur the cats of Mystic Notch into action.

It was like torture waiting for the evening when they were both back at Willa's old Victorian. Pandora suffered through supper and watched as Willa prepared for bed, then made sure the cat door was locked.

"Sorry, buddy," Willa said when she noticed Pandora looking at the door wistfully. "I'm not letting you out, especially not with what happened to the feral cats. I can't risk anything happening to you."

Willa's worried actions touched Pandora and she felt a stab of guilt later that night—after Willa was fast asleep—when she used her escape hatch in the basement.

She made it to Elspeth's barn in record time, not even noticing how the humid night air made her fur fluff out or hearing the peeping of frogs or the hooting of owls on her way. Even the deer that bounded across the trail in front of her could not hold her interest. She had important business to attend to.

The cats were already gathered in the center of the barn. They'd heard what had happened to the ferals and everyone knew it was no accident, nor was it just one of the cat-haters in town.

"So you've heard." Pandora was breathless. "Now you

know we need to take quick action against Danforth."

"Wait a minute." Otis held up his paw. "I just got done telling the others that I've spoken to Ming. He assures me Danforth is not the one. Ming has been with Danforth a long time, and Danforth is good. He's trying to help us."

Pandora could not believe her ears. "Pffft. Help us? I saw him coming up from the church area just this afternoon and he was looking around to make sure no one could see where he was going. He was at the police station that night and had ample opportunity to steal the vial when the big ruckus happened. Not only that, but we know his ancestor was after the vial as well. It *has* to be him."

"Oh really? Is that what your ghost cat told you?" Otis glanced at her skeptically, as if he didn't believe she could talk to ghosts.

The fur on Pandora's back stood on end. She really was getting sick of Otis' attitude. She willed herself to calm down. Soon enough, she'd be able to show him that her way was the right way when she stopped Danforth and saved the day.

"Not in so many words," she admitted. "But he did say that the descendants might be following through with their ancestors' plan. And we all know Miles Danforth arrested Hester because he was after the box. Obsidian said to follow my gut. And my gut is telling me that Danforth needs to be stopped."

Inkspot had padded over to stand between them. "This is no time for arguing." He gave a stern look to Pandora and then also to Otis. "There are many other humans who have ancestors that date back to that time. Miles Danforth was not the only one against Hester. I believe the humans have this under control. We may go in to assist them, but it's not in our best interest to meddle in human affairs unless things become dire. We all know that if we don't let the humans solve this themselves, there could be unpleasant consequences."

Pandora stared at him incredulously. "What do you mean? The feral cats have been poisoned and we are next. After we're gone, there will be no one to protect the humans. That seems pretty dire to me!"

Inkspot nodded. "I know all that. I've communicated with Elspeth. She has made sure that Hope is safely at her human's, but I have sent Kelley to escort Hope to us so that we may protect her this night, which seems to be a critical night of all nights."

"But Danforth needs to be stopped," Pandora persisted.

"Striker seems to have that well in hand."

"Well in hand? He refused to arrest Danforth. He was sitting in the alley watching him and then let him get away! Striker told Hester he was waiting until he had proof! Even Hester said she thought it was him. We don't have time to wait for Striker to wake up to what is going on."

Inkspot sighed. "I know that your instincts are good and I know you are trying to do the right thing, but Striker is right. We do need the proof. And besides, I think it is not as urgent as you believe it to be."

"Not urgent? He's been practicing on the feral cats and we're next!"

"Don't be so impetuous. The old scrolls indicate the extract is most powerful at the source when the moon is at its highest." All the cats looked out the small barn window at the moon. "We have time to wait and be assured we target the right person. Can you honestly tell me that you feel deep down in the innermost part of your soul that Danforth is the one who has the vial? Can you swear that you know that without even the smallest doubt?"

Pandora paused to think about it. She tried to search deep down inside herself. She knew Danforth was up to something, but she had to admit that when she really focused she did have a niggle of doubt about him being the one. Something told her to pay attention to the wisdom of the older cats. Was it possible that she really was too headstrong and impulsive?

She could tell by the way the other cats were looking at her that no one would join her if she decided to go after Danforth. There was only one cat she could depend on now … Hope. But did she dare enlist the young cat to help and risk putting Hope in danger? Hope's magic was very strong and she could use that going up against their enemy, but if anything happened to the two-faced cat, the results could spell disaster for Mystic Notch.

Loneliness settled over Pandora like a black cloud until Kelley's striped face poked its way into the barn. Hope would not be far behind and then she would have an ally to help persuade the cats to take action.

Kelley pushed the door wide and trotted in alone, her head hung low. "I'm afraid I have bad news. Hope is missing."

CHAPTER 14

Tears stung Pandora's eyes as she raced away from Elspeth's barn amidst the protests of the other cats. As she'd feared, they wanted to wait until they had more information. They wanted to take their time and formulate a plan, but Pandora couldn't wait any longer. Her friend was in trouble and she needed to take action.

She took a deep breath and raised her awareness, kicking her already powerful senses into overdrive. Having her senses tuned so highly would use her energy at a rapid rate, but she needed to do it in order to sniff out Danforth's trail. Even though her sense of smell was many times more sensitive than a human's, she still needed the extra boost to be able to locate him from so far away.

She honed in on his scent and followed it to an old

colonial style house huddled deep in the woods. Pine trees had grown up around it, shadowing it in darkness. The house was over three hundred years old and the cedar shingles had turned almost black over time. This was Danforth's ancestral home.

The house loomed over Pandora, gaping at her with sinister, black windows. Not a light was on. No sounds came from it. Pandora's whiskers twitched. Something was wrong.

She circled the house cautiously, sniffing along the perimeter. She could smell Danforth and a cat, which she assumed was Ming, but there was no sign of Hope.

A niggle of doubt bubbled up from her gut. Obsidian's words echoed in her brain,

Follow your gut.

She *was* following her gut. Her gut told her that Oscar Danforth was the one. She'd seen him coming from the church. She'd read the article online about his ancestor accusing Hester of witchcraft and Hester herself even thought it could be Oscar.

But all that information wasn't coming from her gut. That information was coming from technology and observation. Those were the new ways, not the old ways of getting information from inside yourself.

For the first time, Pandora wondered if maybe she *wasn't* doing the right thing. Maybe the other cats were right after all? But then worry about Hope overwhelmed her thoughts. She couldn't just sit back while Hope was missing and in danger. She had to take action and with all the information she had, and the only action that seemed logical right now was to follow Danforth.

She picked up Danforth's trail heading east and followed it, a feeling of dread flowing over her like a heavy, wool cloak.

The trail led to one of the biggest mansions in Mystic Notch—the mayor's house. Pandora's stomach swooped. Were Danforth and Rebecca in on it together? She'd seen them both at the police station and near the church.

Ming had said Danforth was good but you couldn't trust some cats. Just look at how evil the innocent-looking cat, Fluff, was. Ming could be cleverly feeding false information to Otis.

Pandora's nose twitched as she sniffed the air, her heart skipping when she caught the faint scent of Hope mingled with fear. Hope was in there, being held captive.

She hunkered down on her belly and crept closer to the house. The citrusy smell of Danforth grew stronger the closer she got until it overwhelmed all the other scents, almost as if he was much closer than inside the house.

Pandora stopped short. He *was* much closer. She could feel it.

She scanned the area, focusing all her energy on her sight. And then she saw him, crouching behind a forsythia, his attention fixated on the big house.

If Hope was in the house, what was Danforth doing outside?

Her instincts kicked in and she launched herself at Danforth before she could even think to answer her own question.

Pandora landed on Danforth's back, her razor-sharp claws digging in. Danforth wasn't expecting her assault and the force knocked him over onto his face.

"Ow!" Danforth flailed his arms, trying to swat her off.

Pandora dug deeper with three paws, using her forth to pat at his pockets for the vial.

"Hey, what the heck?" Danforth twisted around, dislodging her, his face creased dramatically. "What are you doing?"

Pandora sat back on her haunches and hissed. She hadn't found the vial. His pockets were empty and she wondered what she would have to do to get him to reveal where he had hidden it.

"Of course they're empty. It's because I'm not the one who stole the vial!" he said as if he could read her thoughts. "Of course I can read your thoughts, you foolish feline."

Pandora pulled up short and stood, blinking at the human. *Did he just read her thoughts?*

"Yes, I did just read your thoughts," Danforth said. "And you've got the wrong guy. I could have told you that the other night in the police station if you were receptive. I'm trying to *protect* the cats, not harm them."

Pandora narrowed her eyes. "I don't believe you, I know your ancestor burned Hester to try to get his hands on the extract and you've been trying to get that box from the police ever since it was found."

Danforth's face crumbled. "That's true. Miles Danforth was an evil man, but you can't suffer the crimes of the parents on the children. That's why it was so important to me to get the vial, so I could make sure the cats were safe. To make amends." A tear trickled down his left cheek and Pandora could feel his sorrow and remorse.

Pandora studied Danforth. He *seemed* sincere—in fact, she could feel it. But if what he said was true, then she'd been on the wrong track all along. Could she have been so wrong?

A feeling of dread bubbled up in her chest. She knew Hope was inside that house and if he wasn't telling the truth, then why would he be out here watching the house? If he was in on it with them, then he would be inside.

Too late, Pandora realized that she had made a fatal mistake.

The mechanical sound of the garage door motor caught their attention and the both turned toward it. Danforth made a run for the driveway, but he wasn't fast enough. A black Range Rover whipped out of the garage and Danforth jumped out of the way just before it plowed into him.

Pandora recognized the driver—Rebecca Devon-Smyth. Through the back window, she caught sight of a cat carrier and Hope's two-toned face staring out at her from *inside*.

Pandora's stomach sank. Through her own stubbornness and ego, she'd let the real culprit get away with the extract … and Hope.

CHAPTER 15

Pandora flopped down on the ground in a deep depression. She couldn't believe she'd screwed things up so badly. She been in such a hurry to save Mystic Notch and so sure her assumptions were right that she hadn't taken the time to figure out what Obsidian really meant when he'd said the old ways were powerful and to follow her gut. Now she knew that she should have listened to that niggle of doubt deep down inside and paid more attention to the older cats. But she had been too headstrong, too full of herself. And now Mystic Notch would be plunged into evil and it was all her fault.

"She's got Hope!" Danforth stated the obvious.

"And she plans to do her in," Pandora added.

Danforth's lips pressed together. "Yes, but where is she taking her?"

Good question. Why hadn't Rebecca already used

the extract on her? She must have learned something from her experiments with the feral cats that caused her to hesitate in using it, but what?

A rustling in the bushes caught her attention and she saw Otis' smug face appear in between two shrubberies. Great, just what she needed. It figured Otis would show up now to rub her failure in her face.

She arched her back and got ready for his verbal assault.

"What are you standing here for? Mystic Notch needs your help!" Otis said.

Pandora glared at him suspiciously. "It's too late. I failed us. Rebecca has Hope and the vial."

"I know *that*," Otis said. "If you'd just stuck around long enough like we kept trying to tell you to, you would've known it, too. But that's in the past. We need to move forward quickly. The other cats are still back in the barn formulating a plan, but I know exactly what to do and I need your help."

Pandora didn't know what to think. Was Otis springing some sort of trap to try to make her look even worse than she already did? "I don't believe you. You went against the others and came here on your own?"

"No. They sent me first to scout things out. I took a detour to come here because I knew you would be here."

This only made Pandora more suspicious. Did he really expect her to believe he would go out of his way to help her? She didn't think so. "How did you know I would be here?"

"It was rather obvious to me. I knew your superior

senses would lead you to Danforth." Otis jerked his head at Danforth who appeared to be taking inventory of his injuries.

"But how did you know Danforth would be *here*?"

"As I said in the barn, Ming informed me as to Danforth's intentions. I knew he was trying to protect the vial and that he suspected Rebecca. It was only common sense he would come here to watch her. If you'd only *listened* to us in the barn instead of thinking you knew everything, you would have figured it out, too."

Pandora's heart sank. It was true. She'd been so intent on Danforth being the one that she didn't even look into any of the other suspects or listen to the advice of the cats. "And now I've ruined everything."

"Ahhh, don't be so dramatic. You are just young and impetuous." Otis looked at her and she was surprised to see kindness reflected in his eyes. "Believe it or not, I was just like you once."

"You were?"

"Yeah, but let's not get all sentimental about that now. Mystic Notch is in trouble and you *did* screw up, so get off your keister and help us make it right."

"You still want me to help after what happened?" Pandora's voice was laced with guilt and doubt.

Otis shook his head. "As I've been trying to tell you, Pandora, you have a lot to learn. You do have good instincts. You will be an important member of Mystic Notch, but only if you learn to trust others. You are not a one-man show, you need to take others' input and combine it with your own. I came to get you so that you could have another chance at saving Mystic Notch with all the cats. Surely, you don't want to be left out of that, do you?"

"Of course not, but—"

"Listen, you two, I don't know what is going on, but we need to get a move on if we are going to stop Rebecca." Oscar Danforth vibrated with nervous energy. "My car is a half-mile back on the road … I think she's taking the cat to Hester Warren's land. That's where the lily extract will be most powerful!"

Otis nodded. "We thought so. I have a faster route so we don't need transportation."

Danforth nodded and then sprinted off into the woods. Otis turned and trotted in the opposite direction. "Well, are you coming?" he shot over his shoulder.

Pandora hesitated. She'd lost her confidence and wasn't sure how much help she could be.

"I'm not sure. I don't think you guys need me." A hint of self-pity crept into her voice.

Otis stopped and fixed her with a golden-eyed glare. "That's where you are wrong, young one. This is not about you. This is about the whole of Mystic Notch. We need all the help we can get. Each one of us depends on the other and your presence could be the one thing that tips the balance. But if you prefer to sit here and wallow in self-pity, don't let me stop you."

And with that, Otis turned and raced off into the woods.

CHAPTER 16

Pandora reeled as if she'd been slapped. Otis was right. She'd been a self-centered jerk, thinking *her* way was the only way when she should have been working together with all the cats.

She raced after him at full speed, hoping she wouldn't be too late. Pandora's legs weakened and her energy reserves drained, but she pushed on—Mystic Notch needed her.

She caught up with Otis about a half-mile before their destination. He barely acknowledged her, he was so focused on running, but she thought she saw him crack a quick smile in her direction. Or maybe she imagined it.

She could smell Rebecca's evil intentions well before they got to the site of Hester Warren's house. The foul, rancid stench set her nerves on edge.

When they burst out into the clearing, the moon

was almost at its highest, lighting the area with an eerie glow. A backhoe sat on the east side of the cleared area. A giant oak tree dominated the north. To the south, they'd already started work on the new historical society building—the foundation had been poured, the first floor decking put in place and the studs for the walls erected.

In the middle of the clearing was a smooth spot at the center of which sat a cat carrier.

Rebecca stood beside the cat carrier, her face twisted with evil. In her hand, she held the vial. Moonlight glinted off the silver newt that wrapped itself around the glass. The silvery liquid inside glowed as if it had come to life under the moon. No one else was there.

Otis motioned for Pandora to stop at the edge of the woods before Rebecca noticed them. Pandora fought the urge to rush in and help Hope without thinking things through, as she might have done not that long ago. Maybe she was becoming wiser and less head-strong. She knew waiting was the right thing to do. They needed to maintain the element of surprise.

"Where is everyone?" Pandora whispered to Otis.

"They should be coming soon." Otis glanced up nervously at the moon.

Pandora shifted her weight from left to right, then back again. She could see the side of Hope's face through the metal bars of the cat carrier. Her orange side was in shadow, the black side facing toward Pandora, giving her the illusion of being all black.

Hope sat calmly in the carrier. As Pandora watched, Hope's nose twitched, sniffing the air. Then her head turned toward Pandora like a radar dish homing in on a signal. Their eyes locked. Was Hope trying to communicate something? She got the impression that Hope did not want them to venture further. That she had things under control.

But Pandora couldn't be sure. It would be just like Hope to sacrifice herself for the good of all but Pandora wasn't about to sit back and let Hope do that.

Next to the carrier, Rebecca was extracting the silvery liquid from the vial with an eyedropper. Apparently, her experiment with the feral cats had revealed exactly how much to administer. Further scrutiny of the site told Pandora exactly how she planned to use it, too.

"She has dishes set out with catnip!" Pandora hissed in Otis' ear.

Otis nodded. "She is using Hope as a lure to bring all the cats of Mystic Notch here."

Pandora's heart twisted. Otis was right. Once the cats of Mystic Notch got close enough, they wouldn't be able to resist the lure of the catnip. They would eat it and die. There were only a few cats that could resist the herb's siren song, but they would be no match for evil once the others were gone.

Rebecca bent down, squeezing out a few drops of extract onto one of the dishes then mixing it in with the cat nip. She'd only administered the extract to a few of the dishes. There was still time.

"We need to stop her!" Pandora rocked back on her haunches ready to spring forward, but Otis stuck his paw out in front of her.

"No," he hissed. It's exactly what she wants. We need to be smarter about this. We cannot get too close to the catnip.

"But she hasn't spiked it all yet. The vial is still almost full."

"True, but once you are under the influence of the herb itself, she will easily be able to poison you with the extract. You cannot risk getting too close. We don't know what will happen if the extract is administered undiluted."

Good point. Pandora hadn't thought about that. Maybe there really was something to the older, less spontaneous ways. "But we have to do *something* before it's too late for the others …"

But it was already too late. Pandora could see the other cats racing into the clearing from the woods on the other side. She leaped out of her hiding position to warn the cats, but they'd already ventured too close.

Pandora hissed a warning anyway.

Rebecca whirled around, noticing her and Otis. "Here, Kitty, Kitty," she cooed, as if Pandora would fall for that.

The other cats had put the brakes on, but it wasn't fast enough for most of them. Pandora could already see their whiskers twitching, their necks craning uncontrollably toward the catnip bowls, their noses sniffing wildly.

And all the time, Hope sat calmly in her plastic prison.

Rebecca turned her attention back to the bowls of catnip, squirting the silvery liquid onto the herbs haphazardly.

Some of the cats had already eaten the catnip and were rolling on the ground. Relief flooded through Pandora when she noticed they'd eaten from the bowls closest to them—the ones Rebecca had not yet doused with the extract.

The others were doing all they could to resist the pull of the enticing herb. All except for Sasha. Sasha was immune to catnip. As Pandora fought the pull of the herb herself, she watched Sasha skulk around the perimeter, presumably so she could attack Rebecca from behind.

In her weakened state, Pandora's resistance was low. The herb drew her away from the woods and toward the circle of bowls in the clearing. Otis latched his claws into her tail, trying to pull her back.

Where were the humans? Inkspot had been so sure that Striker had this well in hand. Where was Striker now? With most of the cats looped up on catnip, they could really use his help. She remembered Danforth was also headed this way, but her hopes of the humans enacting some sort of plan to save them were dwindling.

Apparently, Hope *had* a plan in mind. Pandora knew that Hope's special powers had to do with fire. And she saw Hope training her eyes on the new construction. She could feel Hope focusing her entire being in that direction. A flame burst at the corner of the building, lighting up one side of the circle.

As the flame flickered, it cast ghostly shadows of the cats into the circle, their legs and ears appearing elongated as they writhed in a catnip-induced dance. Inkspot wriggled on the ground. Kelley leaped in the air, her bushy tail sticking straight up. Tigger ran in circles.

The fire grew larger, it's crackling heat consuming an entire wall of the building.

Hope aimed again, this time igniting a stack of logs apparently cut from the trees that were removed to clear the area.

Sasha took her chance. She launched herself at Rebecca and landed on her back. Rebecca straightened with a shriek, throwing Sasha off. Sasha landed on the ground and readied for another attack, but Rebecca was faster. She hadn't lost her grip on the eyedropper or the vial and she squirted silvery liquid at Sasha.

The liquid landed on Sasha's side and her fur immediately burst into flames. The sickening smell of singed hair flooded the clearing. Sasha yowled and dropped to a roll.

Rebecca turned her attention to the cat carrier. "Time to make a sacrifice!"

She jerked open the door to the cat carrier, reached in, grabbed Hope by the scruff of the neck and pulled her out roughly. She held Hope up in front of the other cats, whose eyes bulged with terror.

She cackled wildly and clenched her fist tight around the back of Hope's neck forcing her mouth open. She threw the empty eyedropper on the ground and raised the vial up above Hope's head.

Pandora's blood froze. Rebecca intended to pour the liquid straight into Hope's mouth.

Pandora didn't know what the extract would do to Hope, but judging by the way it had set Sasha's fur on fire, she didn't think it was anything good. The liquid amplified energy and with Hope's special abilities with fire, Pandora could only imagine the cat would probably self-ignite.

"No!" Pandora leaped toward Rebecca, intending to knock her down before she could administer the extract.

But Otis was faster. He had leaped a second before and shot out his paw, knocking her out of the way. He landed on Rebecca's shoulder, causing her to drop both Hope and the vial. Hope lay where she fell, apparently exhausted.

Even with the dire circumstances she'd been in, Hope hadn't stopped her fire starting spree. The bulldozer exploded with a loud bang. Trees ignited in flames, one by one. It looked and sounded like a war zone.

A police siren wailed somewhere in the distance. Finally, Striker was coming. Pandora didn't have time to relax, though. Rebecca was crawling on the ground, trying to recover the vial.

Pandora ran forward to stop her, but once again, Otis was quicker. Pandora was surprised at how spry the older cat was. He leapt onto the vial, wrestling Rebecca for possession.

Pandora's heart pounded against her rib cage. She didn't want to jump in the middle and get in the way of Otis' moves, but she desperately wanted to help him, especially since it looked like Rebecca was getting the upper hand.

She watched in horror as Rebecca's fist curled around the vial and then Otis reached out raking his claws down Rebecca's arms. The woman loosened her grip and Otis grabbed the vial with his claw, tipped it to his mouth and guzzled down the liquid.

CHAPTER 17

Otis!" Pandora raced to the calico's limp body, her heart twisting, as Striker's cop car slid into the clearing, followed by Danforth's brown sedan.

"Hold it!" Striker yelled to Rebecca, who had taken off toward the woods.

"Otis, say something!" Pandora screeched, surprised at how much she cared about the old calico. She could still feel the tug of the catnip, but Otis had fallen far enough way that she was able to resist its lure.

A swirl of ectoplasmic mist appeared beside Pandora. Obsidian.

"He's not breathing! He's dead!" Pandora mewled. She was devastated that Otis had sacrificed himself for the good of Mystic Notch … and just when it seemed like they might be friends.

"He's not dead," Obsidian said.

Pandora jerked her eyes away from Otis. "What do you mean. He's not breathing."

"It only looks that way. He is barely taking any breaths. He is *almost* dead, but I can tell from this side that his spirit is not here. He *is* hovering, though ... only something very magical can pull him back now."

"Magical? What do you mean?"

But Obsidian was already fading ... his words just an echo. "Go with your gut."

Pandora wracked her brain for the answer. And then she realized the answer wasn't in her brain—it was in her gut. And in there, she had the same feeling she got when she was sick. The pit of her stomach felt like a leaden hairball was stuck inside it. She wondered if that was how the lily extract felt inside Otis' stomach ... and what she could do to relieve it.

Then it came to her—maybe the medicine in Strikers car would work!

Striker's car was on the other side of the clearing. She would have to go past the catnip at great risk to herself ... but if she didn't try, Otis would die for sure.

Was the medicine magical? She didn't think so. Yet, it was her only hope.

Pandora's eyes slid from the car to Otis. His body was so still, his whiskers wilting. Even his fur had lost its luster.

She *had* to try to save him.

Casting aside all concern for her own safety, Pandora tore herself away from Otis and lurched toward Striker's car. The urge to detour over to one of the catnip bowls was strong, but she resisted, focusing on her desire to save Otis.

Diving in through the open driver's door, Pandora was relieved to see the tube of hairball remedy still on Striker's dashboard. She grabbed it in her mouth and raced back out of the car.

Within seconds, she was at Otis' side, the realization that she'd resisted the pull of the catnip barely registering. Twisting the tube with her claws while gripping the cap in her mouth, she wrenched it open, spit the cap out, pulled Otis' mouth open and squirted almost half the tube of jellylike, brown goo down his throat.

Otis swallowed, then gagged. Pandora's heart fluttered in relief when she saw his chest moving with shallow breaths.

"It's working!" Pandora said.

"Yes, it is," Obsidian replied. "His spirit is withdrawing from this side and moving solidly to the physical plane. He is out of danger now."

Pandora looked at the tube of hairball remedy dubiously. "But this is just hairball remedy that you can buy in the store. It's not magic."

Obsidian shook his head. "You have a lot to learn, young one. It's not the tube that was the magic, it was your actions. You risked your own hide to save one who you used to see as your enemy. *That* was the real magic."

Otis sputtered and coughed, making the most awful retching sounds. He gasped, his stomach heaved, and then out came the biggest hair ball Pandora had ever seen.

"This stuff is gross. What in Hades did you give me?" Otis glared up at her.

"Give you? Why, just the thing that would save your life."

"Save my life? From what?" He glanced down at the half-empty tube of hairball remedy. "Looks more like you were trying to do me in with that vile stuff."

Pandora couldn't believe how ungrateful Otis was acting. "Don't you remember? You swallowed that whole vial of lily extract. You were practically dead until I risked my life to give you this hairball remedy. You must've coughed the extract up with the remedy because you seem to be back to your grouchy self already."

"That's right. I remember now." Otis glanced over at Striker's car then slid his eyes over to Pandora. "I guess thanks are in order, but I see you acted impetuously again, risking a run through the catnip to get to Striker's car. You might well have been harmed yourself. And then where would we be?"

Well, if that didn't beat all. Leave it to Otis to admonish her after saving his life. Pandora almost regretted saving him now, as she second-guessed the feelings of friendship she'd *thought* were starting to develop between them.

But as she studied Otis further, she thought she saw a playful gleam in his eyes, as if he was only playing the part. Maybe he did not yet want to admit that they were allies.

"It appears the lily extract is now gone, thanks to your friend Otis. We can rest in peace." Obsidian bowed at Pandora. "You did good, kid. Thanks." He glanced over toward the woods. "And I see the humans are doing their part, as well."

Pandora followed his gaze. It was almost as if time had slowed down for the humans while she had been busy saving Otis, because Rebecca was just reaching the edge of the woods. Danforth and Striker were fast on her heels.

Rebecca ran toward the giant oak tree, reaching for a low branch. Pandora didn't know if she was planning on climbing the tree or what, but she never made it because Danforth clapped his hand over her wrist and pulled her down. Striker grabbed her other arm.

"Let go of me!" She tried to pull her arms away from the men, but they were too strong. She twisted and kicked, but they easily dragged her away from the tree.

While Striker tried to wrestle Rebecca into handcuffs, Danforth ran to the center of the clearing. He quickly checked the cats, especially Hope, who was still too exhausted to move. Most of the other cats also lay motionless, but Pandora could tell that they were breathing, and even though her heart shattered at the sight of her friends lying there, she had hope they could be saved. Maybe even with the hairball remedy she'd used on Otis.

After checking the cats, Danforth rushed to his car, took out a large, copper box and proceeded to dump the catnip from each bowl into the box. Pandora could feel the seductive pull of the catnip growing weaker as Danforth put more of it in the box. Somehow, the copper must block the effects!

Once enough of it was in the box so that Pandora felt

she would not succumb, she sprang into action. Grabbing the tube of hairball remedy, she ran to the center of the clearing and started administering it to the cats. As she did this, Pandora was vaguely aware of Striker dragging Rebecca to the police car.

"Rebecca Devon-Smyth, you're under arrest for malicious vandalism of town property."

CHAPTER 18

I guess she can kiss her mayor position good-bye," Hattie said two days later.

They were gathered in the bookstore, talking about the fire and destruction of the historical society site, which was big news in Mystic Notch. No one could figure out why Rebecca would set fire to the site. No one knew what to make of her incoherent ramblings about good and evil and magical extracts.

Of course, Pandora knew what had really happened, but most of the humans thought Rebecca had just become unhinged and set the fires.

"You can say that again, and to be blunt, I'm not the least bit upset about it," Elizabeth Post huffed. "Imagine the mayor ruining the new construction of the historical society building like that."

"I guess the devil must have gotten into her." Elspeth

slid a knowing look in Pandora's direction. She'd stopped by the bookstore after picking up from Doc Everett's several of the Mystic Notch cats who had been affected by the catnip, where they'd been kept for observation.

Striker and Oscar Danforth, who had happened along while Elspeth was struggling with the cat carriers on the sidewalk, had stopped to help her and had joined in the conversation. They both nodded in agreement.

"She sure is acting like that down at the police station, talking all crazy," Striker added.

"What is up with the cats?" Cordelia asked Elspeth.

"Oh, just brought them in for checkups." Elspeth covered her lie by bending down to open the doors of the cat carriers.

It had been a minor miracle that none of the cats had perished due to Rebecca's nasty experiments with the celestrium lily extract. All the feral cats had come out of their comas and all seemed to have no adverse side effects. The Mystic Notch cats who had eaten the tainted catnip had also recovered and were back to their old selves. Everything was as it should be.

Inkspot was the first to poke his face out of the carrier. His black coat was shiny and his eyes bright. He nodded to the others and they slowly made their way out of the crates. Kelley cautiously wound her way over to the sunny window, her tail fluffier than ever. Otis nodded at Pandora, then joined Kelley over by the window. Pandora marveled at how Otis had escaped harm. He'd ingested most of the extract and seemed no worse for wear, though Pandora did think his eyes glowed a bit more brightly than before.

Sasha's wounds were the most severe; her left side had been shaved and her skin was pink where it had burned. She favored that side slightly, but shrugged off Pandora's sympathy and headed over to lie in the sun.

Pandora's stomach twisted. It was the first time she'd seen the cats since that fateful night and she was certain Otis had told them how she'd almost screwed things up by jumping the gun and making the mistake of going after Danforth. She couldn't really blame him—*it* was true. Her impetuous actions could have cost Mystic Notch dearly. She had much to atone for.

"What's wrong, Pandora?" Inkspot asked.

Pandora hung her head. "I acted too quickly and it could have cost us."

"Pffft," Inkspot hissed. "I think you are being too modest. Otis told us how your quick action probably saved us."

Pandora's head jerked up. "What?" She glanced over at Otis. What had he told them?

"Yes," Otis nodded. "Take credit where credit is due. I told them all about how your foray to Rebecca's house forced her to speed up the timeline. If your actions hadn't made her run to the historical society site prematurely, she might have done away with Hope before we could stop her."

"But I di—"

"Psst." Otis held up his paw to silence her. "I know your impetuous nature can be problematic, but in this case, I think you combined the new ways and old ways and used them to our advantage."

Pandora was stunned. Otis was giving her credit for

the whole thing when she'd almost screwed it all up. He'd been the one to save them by drinking the extract, but he wasn't boasting about that at all. Her heart melted toward the cranky calico … maybe they would be friends after all.

"But you did the bravest thing," Pandora said to him. "You swallowed the extract so that it can never be used to threaten us again. It almost killed you."

"Meh." Otis feigned indifference. "But it didn't kill me … thanks to you."

"That reminds me." Danforth fished around in his pocket.

"What reminds you?" Willa asked.

Danforth slid his eyes over to the cats and turned red. "Oh, sorry … I was just thinking out loud." He pulled the vial out of his pocket. The silver newt glinted in the light as he held it out to Elizabeth. "I picked this up when we caught Rebecca. She'd thrown it on the ground. I think it should be in the new museum, along with the box it came in."

"You mean you aren't going to try to prove it belongs to your family?" Elizabeth took the vial, obviously pleased.

Danforth shook his head. "Nope. I realize now that it's part of Mystic Notch history."

Elizabeth turned to Striker. "And you're willing to release it to the historical society."

"Yes, Ma'am."

"Well, I just hope there will be a museum to put it in. The site was ruined with the fire." Elizabeth's mouth tightened.

"We're instituting a big fine for that destruction," Striker said. "Rebecca will have to pay it and that money can be put toward rebuilding what was there. And to buying the town a new backhoe."

Willa's forehead creased. "Wait, so *Rebecca* was the one who stole the vial? Why?"

"Actually, it was Felicity who stole it," Striker said.

"Felicity Bates? Why would she do that?" Hattie asked.

Striker shrugged. "I have no idea, but we dusted the box and her fingerprints were on it. She wasn't at the groundbreaking ceremony and she never touched it in the police station that we *saw*. Near as we can figure, she lifted it out of the box when there was that big commotion with the cats that night and no one was paying attention to the box."

Pandora remembered the big chase with Fluff. Felicity had said she'd been in the police station getting papers notarized, but maybe that was just a ruse and she'd ordered Fluff to create a ruckus on purpose so she could steal the vial when everyone's attention was diverted. If that was the case, then Pandora had inadvertently played right into her hands.

Cordelia's face wrinkled up. "So, she stole it *for* Rebecca?"

"Yep. She must have handed it to her sometime after that night," Striker said.

Pandora remembered the flash of red stilettos as they ran out of the police station that night. Rebecca had still been there, probably waiting for Felicity to come out and hand her the vial. They'd planned it all along.

"But *why*?" Josiah asked.

Striker, Danforth, Bing and Elspeth exchanged a look. Striker cleared his throat. "Well, that's where it gets a little sketchy. Apparently, she's a little unstable."

"She always was excitable," Bing said.

"That's right," Elspeth chimed in. "Always going on about her ancestors and how many of them had been mayor of Mystic Notch."

"If you ask me, she relied too much on her ancestors' accomplishments," Hattie said stiffly.

"She did go a little overboard," Danforth said. "According to my genealogy research of the town, Rebecca's ancestor, Nathaniel Phipps, was one of the townspeople that accused Hester Warren of witchcraft back in the 1600s. She became a little obsessed with the whole story and when the box got dug up … well … I guess she went off her rocker."

Cordelia snorted. "I'll say."

Pandora's brow wrinkled. *Rebecca's* relative had accused Hester? She'd thought it had been Danforth's and he'd admitted as much. The article she read online had mentioned two men—Miles Danforth and Nathaniel Phipps. She'd homed in on Danforth and now regretted never getting around to researching things further on the computer.

A vague memory of Willa and Pepper's conversation a few days ago floated up to the front of her brain. Had Pepper mentioned something about Rebecca being related to the Phipps line?

Pandora had been so focused on Danforth, she hadn't paid attention like she should have, too full of her first impressions to get out of her own way. Pandora made a mental note to be more thorough and not so impulsive next time. *Next* time? Yes, she was sure there would be another time when the cats would be called upon to make sure evil didn't take over Mystic Notch.

"So that's it, then. Rebecca just went off her rocker?" Josiah shrugged. "I always thought that woman was a little crazy. Didn't vote for her, either."

"Yep. She was was fixated on the site of Hester Warren's house. Claimed it was her job as mayor to balance out the town or something," Striker said. "Naturally, she's been stripped of the office of mayor and she'll be spending a little time in a mental health facility."

"And what about Felicity? You gonna charge her for stealing the vial?" Elizabeth held the vial up in her hand.

"Can't. We don't have any real proof that she stole it. She'll argue that her fingerprints were on the box legitimately. It would be a waste of the taxpayers' money to even try. And now that it's recovered," Striker shrugged, "I guess it's not that big of a deal."

Cordelia studied Striker with hawk-like eyes. "And just how did you get involved in all this? You're sheriff of the neighboring county. Is there not enough work over there to keep you busy? I know you help Gus out with homicides, but this was hardly a deadly matter."

"Oh, I guess you could say I had a familial interest in the whole affair." Striker's eyes drifted over to the corner where Pandora noticed the ghosts of Hester and Obsidian were swirling around. She knew by their energy that their business here was done and they could finally pass over.

Hester waved to Striker and he gave her a curt nod. Obsidian raised his paw in a final farewell and Pandora echoed the gesture. Then they were gone.

Willa's forehead creased. Her eyes flicked to the corner where the ghosts had just disappeared.

"What were you nodding at?" she asked Striker.

"What?" He turned to look at Willa. "I wasn't nodding at anything … I was just watching a fly buzz around."

Willa whipped around to the corner. "A fly? Where? There are no flies in here. I keep this place clean." Then she turned suspicious eyes on Striker as if she was beginning to realize he was keeping something from her. "And just what do you mean you had a familial interest."

"It turns out Hester Warren was my great great great great great aunt. Or something like that," Striker said. "I'm not sure how many greats, but she was an ancestor so I guess I just kind of took an interest in the case. The box was apparently passed down to her through family lines."

"Wait a minute," Elizabeth said. "So, by rights this vial and the box belong to you."

Striker glanced at Danforth. "Well, I'm not really sure. There's some question as to whose family line it belongs to. The families in this area are so intertwined, it's impossible to tell. Heck, most of us are related in some fashion or another. But if it did belong to me, I would want it to go in the museum."

"And if it belonged to me I would want it in there, too," Danforth said.

"So it's settled, then." Elizabeth was still holding the vial up in her hand. She twirled it around. "But I thought there was something in here when we dug it up. What was it and where did it go?"

"It sure must have been something important if it was kept in that fancy vial and locked away in that silver box," Hattie pointed out.

"Yes, perhaps some sort of a magical potion or elixir," Cordelia added, her eyes sparkling.

Elizabeth frowned at the vial. "That's silly. There's no such thing as magical potions. It was probably just some old perfume or something. If it was anything important, I'm sure the police would know." Elizabeth glanced at Striker.

"Probably just colored water or something. We didn't have it tested or anything so we don't know exactly what it was." Striker glanced at the cats. "And if anyone else does, they aren't telling."

"Well, honestly, it seems like this whole thing was much ado about nothing," Cordelia said. "I mean, it's just an old box."

"Right," Hattie scoffed. "The way Rebecca flipped out and the way everyone was fighting over it, you'd think the box had the fate of Mystic Notch nestled inside."

The two old ladies laughed and everyone joined them.

"I guess that does seem pretty silly. Thankfully, Rebecca's issues have nothing to do with the fate of Mystic Notch, even though she was the mayor." Striker slid his eyes over to the cats, who were all basking in the sun on the windowsill. "And even with her erratic behavior, I'm pretty confident that the fate of our little town is in very good hands."

A Note from the Author

Thanks so much for reading my cozy mystery, "Paws and Effect". I hope you liked reading it as much as I loved writing it. If you did, and feel inclined to leave a review, I really would appreciate it.

This is book 3.5 of the Mystic Notch series. I call it 3.5 because it's a bit shorter and a deviation from the normal series being mostly from the Cat's point of view. I plan to write many more books with Willa, Pandora and the rest of Mystic Notch. I have several other series that I write, too - you can find out more about them on my website *http://www.leighanndobbs.com*.

This book has been through many edits with several people and even some software programs, but since nothing is infallible (even the software programs), you might catch a spelling error or mistake and, if you do, I sure would appreciate it if you let me know - you can contact me at *lee@leighanndobbs.com*.

Oh, and I love to connect with my readers so please do visit me on facebook at *http://www.facebook.com/leighanndobbsbooks*.

Signup to get my newest releases at a discount: *http://www.leighanndobbs.com/newsletter*

ABOUT THE AUTHOR

USA Today Bestselling author Leighann Dobbs has had a passion for reading since she was old enough to hold a book, but she didn't put pen to paper until much later in life. After a twenty-year career as a software engineer with a few side trips into selling antiques and making jewelry, she realized you can't make a living reading books, so she tried her hand at writing them and discovered she had a passion for that, too! She lives in New Hampshire with her husband, Bruce, their trusty Chihuahua mix, Mojo, and beautiful rescue cat, Kitty.

Find out about her latest books and how to get discounts on them by signing up at:

http://www.leighanndobbs.com/newsletter

If you want to receive a text message alert on your cell phone for new releases , text COZYMYSTERY to 88202. (Sorry, this only works for US cell phones!)

Connect with Leighann on Facebook and Twitter:

http://facebook.com/leighanndobbsbooks
http://twitter.com/leighanndobbs

Printed in the USA
CPSIA information can be obtained
at www.ICGtesting.com
LVHW020254170923
758379LV00013B/376